BIXBY TIMMONS AND THE SECRETS OF SHADOW DEEP

BIXBY TIMMONS
BOOK II

By
Dwight D. Karkan

A Tiny Fox Press Book

Tiny Fox Press LLC
North Port, Fl

Never Stop Seeking Great Adventures!

Book one of this series taught me to never give up. Book two is teaching me that mountains move with faith. Keep the flame lit: it only takes one candle to void the darkness.

Thank you to those who keep me grounded. Amber, Selah, Delaney, and Theo for being the pieces to my greatest puzzle. Adam and Paul, thank you for being the iron puzzle pieces that continue to sharpen me. My youth group for always keeping me on my toes.

To Galen and your team, thank you for your continued faith in the Timmons Nation.

CHAPTER 1
SEEKING A WAY IN

"It's not going to work," Tipton replied. His feet were propped up on a hardwood study table, comics sprawled out on the table deep in the heart of Pinnacle Manor.

Bixby didn't even pause as she hissed back at him.

Though Tipton was not an official caretaker of Pinnacle Manor, he loved looking the part. He had become Bixby's sidekick. He wasn't fast, or tall, nor did he have the physical stature to be a traditional sidekick in the comics, but he was what kept her in check when she was about to do something stupid.

It wasn't her red hair, unquenchable curiosity, or ever shortening patience that led her into the next foolish thing she was going to try, but they didn't slow her down either. She simply wanted to know what Cody had in store for her and the other contestants next.

It had been months since Bixby had completed Level One of genius-gone-missing Cody Dragonthorp's elaborate Holo-Riddle. Not knowing when the next level would start could have easily driven her mad if she hadn't found ways to keep her mind busy—which is precisely what she and Tipton were doing now.

Bixby darted in and out of the stacks of the manor's secret library, hoping to find any trace of a secret passageway, trap door, mysterious puzzle box, or stealthily masked code that might yield clues to either Cody's disappearance or even the start of Level Two.

"This one is going to be my best solve yet," Bixby said. She was collecting knickknacks she needed to complete several of the experiments detailed in Cody's hand-written journals—journals which were practically begging her to complete each fascinating entry. Some of them were riddles, while others were detailed experiments.

"We've spent like half a year turning this place upside-down, and all we've managed to do is break things," Tipton replied. "I don't know about you, but I'm sick of getting yelled at. I say we do something else."

"And I say we have to find a way into the next level," she said, throwing a spool of cable over her shoulder. "Plus, name one experiment that hasn't turned out to be awesome in one way or another?"

Tipton looked up from a comic and gazed at her skeptically. "What makes you think that *this* experiment is the key to entering Level Two?"

She didn't have an answer. Not an honest one, at least. So, Bixby made her way past Tipton, set down the massive speaker she was lugging, and reached through his holographic body to flip his comic closed.

"What was that for?" he grumbled.

Since he was visiting as a hologram—his real self wearing a Holo-suit inside a VR launch room miles and miles away— he couldn't reopen the book. It was why he employed the eager to please house H-Bot, Hucklebee, to be his designated page-turner. It allowed Tipton to read through Cody's amazing collection of vintage comics, while Hucklebee pursued joke books to add more one-liners to his already massive digital collection. It was his new *thing*, which Bixby was certain that he was the first robot to have a *thing*.

Bixby began to walk away searching for the next necessity for her latest experiment.

"You know I hate it when you do that, right?" he said loudly, knowing she had to have heard him this time.

Bixby shot a mischievous grin, shrugged, but said nothing.

"I can't wait to say, 'I told you so' when whatever you are doing backfires on you," he replied, irked.

Bixby returned to her work, determined that this would not backfire whatsoever. The current experiment was one dealing with reassembling the library's sound system. It was odd to her that Cody had pulled it apart before his disappearance. Maybe it was nothing.

Maybe it was everything.

"The next riddle could be in a different house setting," Hucklebee chimed in as he assisted Tipton in reading the comic again.

"I have searched every room in Pinnacle Manor in Cody's settings," she replied. "Along with several other settings and found noth–Ouch!"

Hucklebee shot up from the comic. "Are you okay? What happened?"

Bixby nursed the wound. "I'm okay," she answered. "I pinched my finger on the cord."

"Oh, good. I mean not good, but I'm glad it's not serious," Hucklebee said. "Can I be of assistance?"

"Yeah, you can assist me in turning the pages again," Tipton called out. "She'll live."

"I'll get back to you in a minute," Hucklebee said as he made his way to the table and picked up the wire knot.

"No biggie. I've got it," Bixby replied, shaking her head.

"You have been going at these experiments alone for hours. At least allow me to untangle this knot," he replied.

Bixby sighed heavily. She *had* been going at this alone, but only because she wanted to make sure not a single detail was overlooked. The others meant well she knew, but, in the end, she was the one who had to find, get to, and win Level Two. That said, she did come up with a couple of things she could delegate.

"Okay, your options are untangling that wire or taking those speakers and finding their homes around the library. Each spot they need to be put is in the journal. But don't plug in any until I get a chance to look," she said, pointing to said journal that sat on a nearby desk.

"What's the title of this one, again?" Tipton asked.

"'Shake Things Up,'" Bixby replied. She then turned back to Hucklebee. "Which one do you want to do?"

"Can I say both?" Hucklebee asked with glee.

"How about you do one, and then if you finish before me you can jump in?" she suggested, not wanting to squash his enthusiasm.

"Perfect!" Hucklebee chortled as he went to untangle the giant knot.

Tipton huffed, clearly annoyed he couldn't finish the last eight pages of *The Flagrant Shadow*. "What can I do then?"

"Make sure I get these speakers right," she replied.

Tipton rolled his eyes. "Whoopie."

For the next hour or so, Bixby, Tipton, and Hucklebee carefully read each and every line from Cody Dragonthorp's journal, triple checking each step as they went. The location of every speaker was easily verified once they found the first location. They noticed that each spot had hidden connection cables tucked discreetly into the wall.

In all, Bixby and Tipton found eight hidden spots from the very top bookshelf on the very top floor of the library to the wooden doors at the entrance. Bixby envisioned every cable snaking through the walls and making its way back to a grubby receiver that sat on a shelf in the reading area.

Finished with his project, Hucklebee made his walk over to the receiver and started connecting the leads to the back of the metal box. After a few moments, he took a step back with an air of satisfaction around him.

"That's the last one," he called out.

"You're sure you hooked them up right?" Bixby called back.

"I *am* the maintenance robot; I know a thing or two about wiring."

Bixby looked at Tipton, wondering if they shared the same thought. Though Hucklebee was a robot, he was Hucklebee after all; not everything always worked right after he had 'fixed it.'

"I trust you," Tipton said, partly because he believed him, but more so to tease Bixby.

The duo made their way to the ladder. Bixby grabbed the sides, leaned forward, and, using the insides of her shoes, slid down the side rails without ever putting her foot on a rung. Tipton was not as graceful as he slowly bound his way down step-by-step.

Bixby made her way around to the back of the receiver and checked that each wire was exactly as Cody diagramed it, and then again to look for potential hidden codes. Everything seemed to be in order.

"Here goes nothin'," she said, plugging the power cord into the receiver.

A crackle rang out through the library as the archaic system came to life.

"Now what?" Bixby asked.

Tipton looked to the journal. "Now you have to put the vinyl on the turntable."

Bixby cocked her head. "The what?"

Hucklebee provided the answer as he came around an aisle of books. "A record."

"Ah. One of those," she replied, recognizing the black frisbee-looking disc he held in his hands.

"May I?" he asked.

Bixby nodded as she ushered him to the music player. "Sure, but only if you teach me how to use it in the process."

Hucklebee giddily strolled across the library, lifted the glass case that held the steampunk-esque machine, and balanced the sides of the vinyl circle carefully with his fingers as to not damage it. There were knobs on the side and tubes that were now lit up as the system hummed. He placed the record in its now obvious home.

"I think you're going to like this," he replied, almost cooing at the opportunity to bring the system to life.

"You've used one of these before?" Tipton asked.

"Not until now, but I did a quick search while you guys were busy reading the directions," he said with a grin. "It's quite easy to do when you're in fact a cool, walking, talking computer."

"Touché," Bixby replied.

For a moment, the room quieted as Hucklebee placed the needle to the now spinning record. They could feel each note coming from the speakers placed around the library. The music was chirpy and alive, telling their toes to tap and hips to shake to the rhythm of it all.

"Well, it's not horrible," Tipton snarked before working himself up into a little dance on the library floor.

Bixby watched and laughed to the point where her sides hurt. "Where did you get those sweet moves?" she asked with a playful jab.

"Don't be jealous. I've been keeping up with all the trends on the Holo-Connect," he bragged, not slowing in the least.

Bixby wiped the laughter tears from her eyes but couldn't help but be impressed by Tipton's confidence. After another few songs, the record started to skip off the inner edge.

"Time to pick another record," Hucklebee said.

Disappointed nothing ground-breaking had happened, puzzle-wise, Bixby started to spitball ideas. "Maybe there's a secret hidden in a specific one?"

Tipton shrugged. "Maybe. I mean, there's lots of maybes around this place."

"Yeah, I know it's a long shot at this point," she said with a heavy sigh. Bixby thumbed through the album covers over and over. After going through the entire collection a couple of times, she stopped at one that finally caught her eye. "Oh, hello."

Tipton came up to her side, interest piqued. "What'd you find?"

Bixby pulled the record close to her chest but didn't answer. Silently, she turned and walked back to where the record player sat.

"Well?" Tipton insisted. "What's the big secret?"

Still having fun playfully keeping him in the dark, Bixby removed the sleeve from the vinyl and set it aside before placing the disc on its spot.

"Bixby?" Hucklebee asked.

The music was sweet and tinny. Bixby stood there, still quiet, as she was in a trance between the melody and the black circle spinning around and around. After a while, she spoke.

"My grandfather had a poster on his study wall that had the same picture as this record cover. I barely have a memory of it, but I'm certain it's the same picture. It hung behind his desk between his two bookcases that were filled with puzzle boxes and riddle books."

Tipton opened his mouth to press Bixby more about her grandfather but realized now wasn't the right time. That was the most she'd ever spoken to anyone about her grandfather since he'd passed nearly three years ago. Instead, he folded his arms like Hucklebee who was slumped down on the journal, watching her in deep thought.

Bixby was grateful that Tipton and Hucklebee sat quietly at the desk and allowed her to take a few moments to close her eyes and imagine herself there with her grandfather; she missed him every single day.

Nothing good lasted long in Bixby's world, and this was another short-lived moment sealed away for her to revisit later.

"Bixby..." Tipton said.

She didn't turn.

"Bixby..."

This second time, his tone sounded more urgent, but in her mind, she was still standing in Grandpa's den. She desperately didn't want to leave.

"Bixby!" Tipton shouted. "There's another page to this experiment titled 'Final Instruction' but there's nothing written under it. Why would he say there's a final instruction but not have any final instructions?"

Bixby's mind engaged reality at the trembling of the floor beneath her feet. She didn't recall seeing a page that said, 'Final Instructions.'

"That's weird. Cody doesn't leave out details," she replied, thinking back to every element he had put into Pinnacle Manor and Level One of his riddles.

She whirled around ready to spring into action. The floor continued to shake, and the knickknacks on the bookcases started to rattle as she made her way past them. Hucklebee was trying to reread the instructions in their entirety as Bixby arrived at the desk.

"Go back to the last page," Tipton said. "It was there."

Bixby reached through Tipton's hologram, grabbed the journal, and flipped to the end, but there wasn't a single word there: only a blank page.

"You said the words 'final instructions' were written on the page," Bixby said, searching for them.

"I swear, they were just there," Tipton replied.

The glass lid on the record player slowly creaked closed as Bixby made one final, critical realization.

This experiment wasn't like the others; she held the journal close to her face and exhaled heavily.

"He booby-trapped the record player," she said, flustered.

"WHAT?" Tipton and Hucklebee cried in unison.

Hucklebee hesitated, looking like he wanted to go in twelve different directions to do twelve different things. "What do we do?"

"Should I unlaunch?" Tipton asked.

Bixby shook her head, grinning at Cody's cleverness. "I think you'll want to be here for the finale," she replied. "But you're probably going to want to take cover."

At that point, Bixby darted past them and ran for the double doors of the library entrance. Hucklebee followed without question, leaving Tipton at the desk.

"Wait for me!" Tipton cried, racing after them.

The moment Bixby shot through the ginormous wooden doors, she spun around and began pulling one of them closed. "Get the other one!"

Hucklebee obeyed, slamming his robotic hands down on the heavy wooden handles and tugging with all of his might. Since opening the library doors before Level One, the Library gates had never been sealed.

Tipton, still running full tilt, hadn't quite made it out yet and it was plainly obvious he wasn't going to before they sealed him in.

"No!" he shouted. "Wait!"

"You're a hologram, Tipton," Bixby shouted. "You'll be fine!"

"I have the Holo-Riddle Suit on!" he shouted as he began to stumble.

Bixby's eyes widened in panic; with a Holo-Riddle Suit on he could feel pain and was now wobbling out of control towards the doors that Bixby couldn't stop from closing.

"Unlaun—" was all she could get out before the world around them exploded.

CHAPTER 2
AVOIDING TROUBLE

The blast ripped the air from Bixby's lungs. She spent the next several moments on her back, trying to catch her breath. She'd even slid a few feet on the cold, hard floor and wound up near the base of the stairway that led to her room.

Tipton moaned somewhere nearby.

"Tipton?" she asked aimlessly, coming out of her daze. "You okay?"

She sat up, rubbed her eyes to clear her blurry vision, and found her friend pressed up against the wooden entry, unmoving.

"Oh no. No. No," she muttered over and over. As quickly as her aching body would allow, she pushed herself up.

Hucklebee made an appearance and knelt next to her. "Are you okay?"

The ringing in her ears made it hard for her to understand, but she managed. "I'm fine," she replied. "But Tipton hit that door, hard."

"Tipton didn't hit the door... that did," Hucklebee said as he put his shoulder into pushing open the half-closed library doors to reveal the wreckage inside.

Bixby's eyes shot wide open, and her stomach started to turn at the sight of the state of the library—not to mention the sight of Tipton laying just inside the entry, partially obstructed by a ton of books.

Hucklebee helped her to her feet, and, in turn, they both rapidly made their way over to Tipton who had by then rolled over. She pushed the mountain of books away from him while he was trying to sit up. Bixby slumped down beside him as they both took inventory of the disaster around them.

"I told you so," Tipton said. He tried to let out a small chuckle, but it quickly turned to a wince of pain.

He did indeed predict this outcome, but Bixby was more concerned that she'd finally done something stupid enough to get them hurt.

"You got any ideas on how we are going to clean this up?" Tipton asked, surveying the ruined library. Every bookshelf had fallen over on itself. Books by the tens of thousands were all over the floor. The several hundred-pound wooden desk that sat in the middle of the library was flipped over on its side. Surprisingly though, the record player and record were still spinning on the turn table where Bixby had left them.

She sat there perplexed at his question because she had no idea what to do next, which was a strange place to be for Bixby.

"It does explain why it was called, 'Shake Things Up,'" Hucklebee said, filling the silence and making the connection between the title and the damage.

Bixby carefully made her way over to where she put down the record's cover; she wanted to keep that memory close if it wasn't already destroyed.

"How did you know it was going to blow up the library?" Hucklebee asked, helping her rummage through the mess.

Bixby spotted the journal on the floor near where she was searching, picked it up, and turned to the final page of instructions.

Bixby held up the instructions. "Read," she said as she turned around to search again for the record's sleeve.

"What are you talking about?" Tipton said over Hucklebee's shoulder. "It's all blank."

"Lucky for us, I know a few things about hidden words. Try to apply something warm, like Hucklebee's breath or arms on the page," Bixby encouraged.

Tipton's mind raced back to when Hucklebee sat with his H-bot arms draped over the journal while watching Bixby listen to the record.

"What are you waiting for, Hucklebee?" Tipton urged.

Hucklebee hunched near Tipton and breathed his hot computer air onto the pages in hopes of seeing what would happen to the emptiness inside the leather journal.

"Final Instructions," Tipton read aloud as the words began to appear, and almost immediately fade. The words were then gone, once again.

"Invisible ink?" Hucklebee asked.

Bixby nodded and beamed. "Activated by heat."

Hucklebee quickly huffed as hard as he could onto the page to read the rest of what was hidden.

"Not cool, Cody," Tipton said as he glanced down at the final instructions.

ONCE THE FIRST SONG PLAYS,
YOU WILL HAVE TEN MINUTES TO RUN.
ALL ELSE WILL BE HIDDEN.

"You two are lucky you have me around or you would've been inside when this thing went off," she huffed, looking around. She dropped down to her hands and knees, sifting through wreckage for the vinyl cover like the one in her grandfather's study.

"I still was," Tipton said with no small amount of snark as he too searched for the lost item.

"You could have told me you were wearing your Holo-Riddle Suit," Bixby replied.

Bixby gave him the Holo-Riddle Suit that she wore in Level One so that he could make a replica for himself before sending hers back.

"I have been trying to figure out how to make being a hologram as realistic as possible in the real world," Tipton replied.

In his attempt to program the coin to make him less like a ghost and more like a hologram that was really there, he coded his launch room to make him go around obstructions. The coin, paired with a copy of Cody's Holo-Riddle Suit design, made him feel more and more like he was actually at Pinnacle Manor.

In the panic of the imminent blast, Bixby forgot that his coin would make him stop at the closing door versus being able to ghost right through it, and she was shocked that he was wearing the Holo-Riddle Suit. She was trying to convince herself that because she didn't know he could feel pain, then technically it wasn't really her fault he got banged up, but her logic wasn't helping much.

"Why would he put the last instructions in invisible ink?" Hucklebee wondered, not concerning himself with the shortcomings of Tipton's inventions.

"I think Cody is trying to keep something hidden down here," she replied, pausing her search for the vinyl's cover to look for any signs of hidden doors or clues that had potentially been revealed after the explosion.

"Like the knowledge of how to make sound waves into a bomb?" Tipton grumbled. He drew short and waved Bixby over to the pile he was examining. He pointed to a record sleeve peeking out from the bottom of the heap.

"Or to keep people from finding what he is trying to keep secret down here," she replied. She then bent over and picked up the undamaged cover. "My Grandpa used to tell me that the best way to hide a secret is to erase it from everywhere but the mind, even though the mind is the most dangerous place to keep a secret because it will always try to get out. The real question is, 'What secret was Cody trying to hide?'"

Tipton gestured at the mess all around them. "Again... a sound bomb."

Bixby and Tipton's thought processes behind why Cody would blow up his own library aligned with each of their passions. For Tipton, it had to be science related, and for Bixby the blast must have been something to do with Cody's grand riddle. Bixby realized that they couldn't know either way, so she changed the subject.

"But it was pretty cool," she chuckled in return. "Besides, I had Hucklebee scan the entire library and remember where everything went as soon as we found this place."

"Cleaning up this mess will have to wait," Hucklebee said, standing at attention.

Tipton squinted unsure of what he meant. "Why?"

"Because Harvey is looking for me," he responded. "He sent me a message asking why the manor just shook."

"Which means my parents will ask the same question," Bixby groaned. She knew they'd find fault in her doing Cody's experiments even though nobody could predict the outcomes – especially ones like leveling the library. Her only prayer was that it wouldn't lead to being grounded... again.

"I'll let them know we're okay, and that we are headed upstairs," Hucklebee replied.

For Bixby, the stairs seemed much steeper knowing that her mom and dad would be waiting for them on the other side of the fireplace in her room. The shock wave must have been much bigger than she originally thought, because the fireplace was pushed closed in the locked position meaning her parents were unable to go down and check out the damage. That wasn't necessarily a bad thing considering the state of things down there. With a huff, she popped the latch up and pushed open the fireplace, to be greeted by two frowny-faced parents and Harvey's usual scowl. They were generally okay parents to have as a teenager, but they'd become more guarded since the ending of the last level and Bixby's newfound knack for breaking things.

"Mom, what happened to your shirt?" Bixby blurted out, looking at her mom who was covered in what she could only guess was sweet Miss Marmalade's delicious hot cocoa.

"Oh, I don't know Bixby. Maybe I was enjoying myself when a giant explosion startled me so bad that I spilled my hot chocolate all over me," she replied, eyebrows furrowed and voice growly. It was the voice her mom made right before she blew her lid, so Bixby knew for certain she was walking on eggshells at the moment.

"Care to tell *us* what happened?" Mr. Timmons added.

It was hard to take her father seriously when he was petting a holographic baby polar bear that was sitting next to him like a pet dog.

No way, was all Bixby could think at the sight of the Holo-Gloves on his hands. Her body tried desperately not to reveal the excitement that was bubbling up inside her like a shaken soda can. He had been working on those gloves to complement Tipton's coin and the Holo-Riddle Suit. If she had a pair, Tipton wouldn't be a ghost hologram anymore, but more of a tangible object with which she could interact.

The questions in her head kept coming: What does a baby polar bear's fur feel like? Would I stop walking through Tipton's hologram? Can Dad make me a whole suit?

"Well?" he pressed.

Focus Bixby, she thought, snapping back to the reality of the situation. She had become really good at telling the truth, just not the whole truth, and even better at making that truth sound like not such a big deal.

"Well, we were reading one of Cody's journals that he hid in his library. He left detailed instructions on how to rebuild the record player system. We followed all of his instructions to the letter, and it worked, until we realized that he had booby-trapped the system to create some sort of sonic boom."

Her dad pressed his lips together as he thought about it for a moment. "Sonic booms only happen when you break the sound barrier," he eventually said. "But I've heard about the premise that lower frequencies paired with their equal high frequencies create very strong sound waves."

"Yeah! Exactly! We realized the trap was triggered too late, so we couldn't stop it, but it was pretty cool to see how Cody used eight speakers placed in the exact right spot, at the exact right angle, at the exact right frequency, based on the acoustics of the library, to make such a huge noise."

"That *is* pretty impressive," he said.

Bixby glanced at her mom, who clearly understood that Bixby's attempt at distracting her dad was being made in order to avoid punishment. She had navigated the situation almost perfectly. Her final move was to pull the 'I could have been hurt' card, but it had to be done well or they wouldn't let her go down to the library again.

Simple miscalculation Mom. It won't happen again, was all she needed to relay. She sulked a little as she began to speak. "Honestly, if we didn't realize it when we did, our ears would still be ringing," she said, knowing they'd dodged something much worse. Bixby slumped down on the end of her bed dramatically for more effect.

Her mom, thankfully, seemed to buy into it. "Are you alright?" she asked, looking Bixby over from head to toe.

Bixby could barely mask her relief. *It's working.*

"I'm fine, Mom, really. And I promise we had no idea it was going to do any of that," she said.

"How is the library?" her dad asked.

Bixby felt her heart jump. "Um, just knocked a few things off the shelf," she said, trying to sound calm. "No biggie. We'll tidy it up."

As her dad eyed her, probably trying to gauge whether or not to fully believe her, Bixby's mom was the one who found the hole in her story.

"You keep saying 'we,' yet you are the only one in this room," her mom said. "Care to explain that?"

"Oh, well umm…" Bixby started unraveling. *Stupid Bixby,* she thought. *Way to slip up on that.*

Her dad snapped to attention. "Tipton!"

From behind the door, the husky boy bashfully emerged. His face was glowing beet red.

"Hucklebee had better be there with you Tipton, or I may be testing my new Holo-Gloves on your hologram," he said, flexing said gloves as Tipton's eyes grew wider than dinner plates. Bixby couldn't tell if he was shocked at the completion of the gloves, or terrified that her dad might actually be serious about testing them out around his neck.

Bixby was indeed getting older, so her dad had created a new rule that let Bixby have a little more access to her new best friend as long as Hucklebee was with them. That meant that Tipton no longer had to get written permission to launch in during "visiting hours" to Pinnacle Manor, but he wasn't a fan of the secrecy. Not one bit.

"He is," Harvey replied, leaning against the bookcases near her door. Harvey was the house program that oversaw everything that happened at Pinnacle Manor. He was what made Pinnacle Manor the most unique home in the world. With the help of Tipton, Harvey was also able to turn his program into a Holo-Body like Tipton's.

Harvey knew that Hucklebee would not be far behind when there was excitement to be had.

"Oh, hi everyone," he said, stepping out from behind the door. "I was just back here fixing this squeaky hinge."

"You're a terrible liar," Harvey replied. "We all know your programming makes you one."

Bixby's mom shot her an amused look before clearing her throat. "Besides the sonic whatever, is everyone okay?" she inquired.

A trio of, "Yes, ma'am." "Yes, mom," and "Yes, Mrs. Timmons," belted out at the same time.

"Good. In the future, could you please be a little more careful, or Tipton will not be allowed over without a parent's supervision?" she asked, knowing that they would all say yes, but they could tell that she was worried about them, rather than wanting to actually follow them around on their adventures.

Everyone nodded *yes* in response.

"Tipton, are you planning on staying for a virtual dinner?" she asked. "I can set you a spot at the table, and you can eat whatever you've got with us."

"If it's okay with you and Mr. Timmons," he said bashfully, not wanting to eat alone. Sure, he'd still be in his own launch room eating the dinner he had made and brought in his launch room when it came down to it. Virtually was better than what he had in real life, and the company was pretty good as well.

Bixby's dad leveled a finger at her and Tipton. "And know that just because I think the experiment was cool, doesn't mean I'm not watching you two like a hawk. You know what I'm saying?" he asked, pointing two fingers at his eyes and then pointing them back at the pair.

"Yes sir," they replied in unison.

Bixby then tensed and held her breath, wondering when the grounding was coming.

"Dinner is in fifteen minutes. Please wash up," Miss Marmalade chirped from the hallway.

"Oh, goodie," Mr. Timmons cheered like a child at the unexpected sound of the dinner bell.

The family was always in for a treat on the nights Miss Marmalade cooked because she had access to the entire world of food and the skill to make anything perfectly the first time. Normally, Bixby was saving one of her mother's terrible meals or keeping the dessert carts stocked, but on surprise dinner night Miss Marmalade's full range of culinary skills was on display. It was the perfect announcement to break the tension in the room.

"Plus, I think there are two unattended toddlers back in the Great Hall, most likely pulling things out of the Christmas tree," Harvey replied. Bixby was certain he could digitally see her younger brothers doing just that.

It worked, Bixby thought in her head as confetti cannons went off in her mind. She finally was able to avoid getting grounded.

Mr. Timmons ushered his baby holographic polar bear and Mrs. Timmons out of the room,

"Guess I need to change my shirt," her mom grumbled as she left the room. "And I loved this blouse."

A reminder came from Bixby's dad before he too made his way down the hall. "Oh, speaking of the twins pulling things out of the Christmas tree, another package arrived for you Bixby. I put it in the tree high enough that they wouldn't get to it."

Bixby shot Tipton a grin. Neither of them had ever had a real Christmas tree before.

Harvey had finished uploading Hucklebee's chore list to attend to after Tipton left for the night. What Harvey didn't know was that Hucklebee had also offered to spend the night restoring the library to its pre-explosion state. Bixby knew she would have to secretly help cover some of the slack for Hucklebee, but, even so, the experiment was well worth it.

"Harvey! It's been so long since we've seen you looking all dapper in your Holo-Body and snazzy outfits," Tipton said, motioning toward him.

Harvey spent most of his time as the digital program that oversaw the shifting, shaping and overall care of Pinnacle Manor. Thanks to Tipton's ingenious coin that let him project into Pinnacle Manor, Harvey could also take the holographic presence of his choice. He loved launching in a traditional old Scotsman Holo-Body, wearing his flat cap, khaki pants, white button-up shirt with a wool vest, and jacket with the elbow patches sewn in. If every word he said wasn't as crass as it was normally, he would be a loveable spry grandfather.

"It is the Christmas season after all," Harvey said with a radiant bow. His jovialness took everyone by surprise, but his recent absence had not gone unnoticed.

"So...where have you been lately?" Bixby asked.

"System reviews and basic holiday prep," he replied. With that, he spun around and started for the door.

"Hey! Wait!" Bixby shouted, stopping him short. She had a feeling there was more to it than that. "Is something wrong? You can tell us."

"Nothing is wrong, I assure you."

"Well, if there was, we're here to help."

Harvey made a nod with his cap. "Thank you."

Then he was gone.

Tipton twisted his mouth to the side and scratched his head. "Man, that was weird," he said. "Wonder what's bugging him."

"No idea, but seeing how he's been gone more than not, something has to be up," she replied. She then turned to Hucklebee. "Do you know anything?"

"Sorry guys, when I plug into the system, it is a one-way thing. Harvey uploads everything I need to my hard drive, but I normally can't see back into his system. All of the data I receive is pretty basic, chores lists and daily to-dos, nothing out of the ordinary," Hucklebee said as he plopped down in Bixby's new egg chair by the fireplace.

"Well, if you get a chance, dig around a little and see what you can find," Bixby said as she washed her hands in the bathroom sink.

"Understood," Hucklebee replied.

"Since detective Hucklebee is now on the case, let's eat," Tipton said, grinning. The smell of dinner had crept down the hallway and into the room, and if it was half as good as it smelled, Miss Marmalade had outdone herself.

CHAPTER 3
THE INVITATION

It took the three troublemakers a few minutes to wash up and make their way towards the kitchen. It would take them a few minutes longer after seeing the spectacular sight of the Great Hall for the first time; they ogled the impressive display of lights and holiday festivities.

"Whoa!" Tipton gasped. "Have you ever seen anything like this?"

Bixby had no words.

Harvey had put up the display earlier in the day while the trio was in the hidden library setting up their experiments. It was a remarkable sight based on any standards, let alone for two teens who came from nothing.

"In my house, we are lucky to get a tree up before Christmas Eve," Tipton said as he ogled the snack cart that was left in the middle of the room.

"My old house was too small for us to have a tree. Instead, we would always cut one out of an old cardboard box if my dad could find one big enough. I would spend all day coloring it green, and when Dad got home, we would punch holes in it and hang the ornaments my grandparents gave us. It was nothing like this," she said as she stared in awe at the sparkling old trinkets finally hanging from real tree branches.

"Harvey has never gone all out like this before, especially without my help," Hucklebee said, inspecting the decorations on the mantle of the fireplace. "Can programs suddenly become sentimental?" he asked his companions.

Hucklebee's question raised more suspicion about what was bothering Harvey, but everyone decided to let it be for the time being as Bixby found her way to the ornately wrapped package tucked on a tree branch. Her dad was wise to put it up high enough that the twins couldn't reach it.

"Who is it from?" Tipton asked.

"I don't know; it doesn't say," she said, looking at the tag written with exquisite detail. "Only that it's to me."

The gift was no bigger than a toddler's shoe box. It was wrapped in festive, shiny green wrapping paper neatly secured by a golden ribbon tied in a perfect bow. As Bixby continued to inspect the box, she was sad that she would have to eventually open it. Noticing that it weighed next to nothing, she wondered what could possibly be inside. She gave it a shake but heard nothing.

"I've received packages from fans with puzzle boxes and trinkets reminding me of Level One, but nothing as beautiful as this," she said.

"Open it already," Tipton urged.

"Bulldog scanned it, so it has to be safe, right?" she said to herself. 'Bulldog' was a name Bixby only used for Arthur the security H-bot when he wasn't around. Though he was a strict keeper of rules, order, and efficiency at Pinnacle Manor, it was nice to have him at Pinnacle. She felt like she had her own Secret Service agent, which was sometimes good to feel safe, and sometimes a real pain when she wanted to go off-script around the manor.

Confident that there was no danger, she gave the ribbon a little tug. It effortlessly pulled apart revealing a wax stamp with a castle pressed into it.

"Curious," she said.

Carefully running her finger along the seam where the wax circle set, Bixby took care not to ruin the seal. As she pulled the paper back to uncover a plexiglass cube, she gasped at the miniature scene inside.

"No way," she whispered, pulling the cube close to her face to get a better look.

She could see an ornate little castle sitting on top of a hill. It looked like something out of the Renaissance Festival that she and her family attended almost every summer. Horse-drawn carriages were going in and out of the front gate as they dropped guests off at the front door. In the square, it looked like the townspeople were celebrating something, but inside the private castle gate, guests were dressed in fancy clothes and wearing fancy masks that hid their entire face. Snow lightly covered the ground and the peaks of all the exposed surfaces. The castle itself was lit up like Bixby's new Christmas tree. Every window was emitting a warm glow. Just then, all the townspeople looked towards the sky inside the cube. Bixby was also drawn to the fireworks show that had begun. In every color of the rainbow, the light show started to spell out words.

Find My Home By December 23rd

"What does it say?" Tipton asked again peering over Bixby's shoulder.

"Is it a puzzle box?" Hucklebee asked.

"Is it the start of Level Two?" Tipton added.

Bixby held the cube for all to see. "I'm not sure, but it clearly has a timer."

Tipton scanned the cube, took a video with his Holo-Writer, and started searching immediately.

"What's today's date?" Bixby asked.

"December the twentieth," Hucklebee answered.

Bixby nodded and continued to watch the mesmerizing fireworks. "So, that gives us less than four days to figure this out."

"Maybe Pippa could help?" Tipton offered.

Bixby immediately paused her thought as a mischievous grin slowly crept across her face.

"What?" he asked.

"You and Pippa seem to be getting pretty close," Bixby said.

Pippa was a girl who went to Holo-School Prime with Bixby and Tipton. Bixby had noticed that she'd been taking a lot of the same classes as Tipton because of their love for programing and everything Cody. However, Bixby had a hunch that their friendship was a little bit more than 'like.'

"Can I send it or not?" he asked again, a little irked.

Bixby thought about the request. She didn't really trust anyone outside of herself, Tipton, and the inhabitants of Pinnacle Manor. The last time she let someone else in, Mad Maggie Murdock tried to push her off a mountain, and that was after she had thumped her over the head and tied Bixby to a cot. Needless to say, those two events had put Bixby on edge.

"Alright, look. I'm sure she's very nice and extremely skilled, but I really want to keep this cube a secret from the outside world for a little while longer," Bixby said. "Nothing personal."

"Your loss," he said with a shrug. "I'm pretty sure she's Marshall Grooves' insider to finding anything on the web. She could find that castle in a flash, and if she can't, that's because it doesn't exist."

"Why Tipton, you seem rather fond of the girl," Hucklebee said. "And given your changing skin color, I'd say there's a lot of affection there, too."

Bixby giggled.

"Knock it off," Tipton grumbled. "You're reading way too much into this."

"Are we?" Bixby teased.

She was going to say something else when her stomach growled. It was an instant reminder that dinner was waiting, and she needed to show the box to the rest of her family. Each moment closer to December 23rd without getting closer to answers was a moment of wasted time.

Once in the kitchen, Harvey was the first to reach the box since he was the house system, and most likely overheard the entire conversation. Bixby could tell he was scanning the cube right from the start.

"No noticeable marks or hidden words," he said.

"What is it?" Mrs. Timmons asked as she arrived with the rest of the family to the kitchen island.

"I'm not sure if it is an invite or a riddle." Bixby set the cube down on the middle of the countertop.

A moment later, Mrs. Timmons groaned when revelation struck. "Oh mercy. It's Level Two."

"Or an invite to a party," Hucklebee suggested.

Mr. Timmons intently watched it play through a second time, and, upon the completion of the fireworks show, he asked, "Is there anyway we can scan and find the castle? Assuming it is Level Two, there have to be hundreds or thousands of castles out there. How would we know where to go?"

"I've already begun our search for this castle," Arthur replied from the back of the crowd. That was the efficient response Bixby had expected from him. She looked at the other H-bots in the room huddled around the cube.

"Just you?" Bixby asked Arthur.

"Well, myself and the other H-bots," he admitted. "Do sit down and eat while our work progresses."

Bixby could tell they were indeed searching because if she looked closely at each of their eyes, there was a slight twitch like they were reading between entire pages of material in microseconds.

"I'll let you know if anything comes up," Miss Marmalade patted Bixby on the back and handed her a plate full of tonight's surprise meal. "I promise."

"I'm not sure I'm hungry anymore," she replied, feeling her stomach churn as the words played over and over again in her head.

Level Two.

Chapter 4
Same School, Different Bully

Bixby had one day left until Christmas break, and she planned to spend her last few hours at school between making her Christmas list and staring at the digital image of the cube she had on her Holo-Writer. It would be easy to pull off because most times her teachers had them doing Christmas-related homework problems like:

If Santa Claus leaves the North Pole and travels a thousand miles an hour between each house around the world, and only half of the houses in the world have good little girls and boys, how long would it take Santa to deliver all the presents?

Bixby liked these questions because there were so many variables that the math teacher would leave out. She could simply answer:

Not enough information. How much does the sleigh weigh? What is the exact distance between each house? How long does it take reindeer to accelerate from 0—1,000 mph?

Every year she received an A- on her work because technically she was right about the need for a whole gob of more data to come to a definite answer. Her teacher usually added the minus because it defeated the purpose of festive math problems when she took all the fun out of it.

"What are you doing?" Tipton leaned over and tried to peek at Bixby's Holo-Writer.

She yanked it away from his prying eyes.

"If you must know, I am finishing my Christmas list," she said, sounding a little bashful. She was really far behind on her list and planned to give it to her parents today.

"You still make a Christmas list? I thought everyone just asked for money and gift cards," Tipton said. "In case you want to shop for me, I need a new set of Gromit sockets to build all of the new gadgets for the next level." He grimaced as the word "level" escaped his mouth.

Bixby was sure that if Greg and Wesley got a cube, they would've already confirmed it with each other, but she didn't want to make it public knowledge with the world just yet. In doing so, her life became more hectic with people bombarding her with requests for autographs, interviews, and the general annoyance of questions.

He quickly continued, "A case of Uncle Yuki's Tickle Tarts and warm socks; my feet get cold in my Launch Room."

She could hardly blame Tipton, though, because the Christmas list she was working on was, in reality, a front for what had been living rent-free in her head all day: the castle in the cube. Doing her best to hide the anxiety, she gave him a turn and a shake of the head, but not at his slip up.

"Tipton... you still eat Tickle Tarts? What are you, like six?" Bixby asked, continuing her Holo-Search for a puppy.

Tension avoided.

"Tickle Tarts are good at any age. I can't help it if one of the finest foods in the world is marketed towards elementary-aged children. I will probably be eating them until the day I die," he said with an unapologetic look.

"Which is probably going to be any moment if you two clowns don't shut up," said a voice from behind them as Bixby felt the thud of someone thumping the back of her padded chair.

Neither Bixby nor Tipton had to turn around to know who the threat came from. During Level One of last spring's game, which almost claimed Bixby's life, Bixby had exchanged harsh words with, threw a brick at, was threatened by, and even physically tackled Wesley Dagger. Because the rules of the Riddle stated that they cannot talk outside of the Riddle, Wesley's sister Penny Dagger and her band of misfit hackers had taken to heart the task of making Bixby's school day a living nightmare.

"I'm talking to you two freaks," she said.

"And we are ignoring you, Penelope," Bixby replied as she continued her search, knowing that Penny hated when people called her by her given name.

"You think you're really funny, don't you?" Penny replied.

"Listen, Penelope," Bixby said her full name again slowly to make sure every syllable harshly got on her last nerve. "You seem like a really nice person and all, but, you see, I'm allergic to bullies and mean people. Every time you show up, I get this itch on my shoulder," Bixby said as she reached up, and, with a flicking motion, brushed her shoulder off as if she were telling Penny to shoo. "There it goes again, which means I'm going to need you to leave now before…"

Bixby pulled a strand of her red hair to her mouth and started chewing on it. Last year when Wesley called her soulless for having red hair, she informed them it was red because she would wash it regularly with the blood of her most recent victims. It was gruesome to say out loud once, but now all she had to do was chew on her red hair and everyone knew what she meant.

The gesture had never failed to get a conversation to end, or at least switch directions. This time, knowing it didn't faze Bixby, Penny turned her ire towards Tipton who was a little less confident in standing up to her.

"While you're shopping for your tubby friend, how 'bout you pick up a nice first-aid kit for him, because one of these days he is going to launch into school, but instead of being in his seat, he'll be out back behind the field house where I'm going to pummel the porker," Penny said as she sat back in her seat.

Tipton slouched nervously in his chair knowing her hacking skills were extremely high on the "Epic" scale.

"See you after enrichment, Tipton," Bixby said as if the threat was not worrisome at all. "Don't sweat her; if you launch in and find yourself behind the field house, just unlaunch. She can't do anything on school grounds to hurt us."

Then Bixby looked over her shoulder at Penny while tapping on her Holo-Writer a few times and said, "Ah, there you are Penelope Dagger: I'm sorry to inform you that Santa has taken you off his 'Naughty List' because even the coal doesn't deserve to have a bad Christmas with you."

Penny clenched her jaw, mashed her lips together, balled up her fist, and shook her head as the bell rang and the room went dark.

For the next two hours, Bixby completed a range of tasks, including physical and mental workouts. The school would not let her bring in outside work like the castle invite into her enrichment time, so she focused on the task-at-hand knowing that she needed to be at her best by the twenty-third. Last spring, she discovered what poor physical shape she was in during Level One. To fix that, with Harvey and occasionally her mother's help, Bixby was dedicated to training hard. For the first hour, she completed physical fitness routines, which included running, climbing, jumping, pushing, pulling, lifting, and everything in between. One of her other competitors who became an ally at the end of Level One, Marin St. James, had sent her a link to the workout enrichment that she was using at military school. At first, Bixby hated every minute of the first hour, but now she could feel herself getting stronger. Most days when the hour was up, she was shocked at how quickly time had passed and wanted to keep going. But she also knew she needed to keep sharpening her mental skills as well, so the second hour was focused on riddles. If it were not for Bixby's family and quick thinking, she may not have been able to solve all of the challenges she had been given. The mental aspect was just as important as the physical. Today she was solving complex Sudoku puzzles. Each row and column of the puzzle had to have the numbers one to nine in any given order, but she couldn't repeat a number anywhere in the row, cube, or column. As she was writing in the last column of numbers, her Launch Room went dark: time's up.

"Sugar... I had that one, too," she whispered to herself as the Launch Room lights came back up and the door opened.

"You're getting faster each day, Miss Timmons. You are even surpassing what I thought you were capable of doing," Arthur said in his monotone voice, standing near the room's control panel.

"Is that your way of giving me a compliment?" Bixby asked.

"Yes. And I am guessing not calling me the Bulldog is your way of being nice to me as well, Miss Timmons?" Arthur asked in return.

Bixby laughed. "I guess we're both trying to be more civilized, aren't we?"

Arthur nodded. "I suppose I can get used to these verbal niceties, but don't ask for extra bedtime privileges. I draw the line there."

"Understood," Bixby replied. "So, any luck on the castle?"

"I'm sorry, Bixby, but the search has come up empty for now," Arthur replied, sounding disappointed."

"But you're still looking?" she asked.

"Of course, Bixby; we have taken turns sitting with the cube and running tens of thousands of algorithms on it. I promise that you will be the first to know if something comes up."

It was the second time an H-bot had said "I promise," but it didn't make her feel any better that the clock was still counting down.

"Thanks."

She then pulled up her Holo-Writer as she walked toward the Great Hall and texted Tipton.

M get a cube?

The rules stated that Bixby could not talk to her only ally, Marin directly. In the spirit of having Penny help Wesley harass Bixby, Bixby was using Tipton as her go-between to communicate with Marin. It was easier to call her "M," so as to not officially break the rules.

Tipton was usually really good with communication, so it was not a surprise when he immediately responded.

Tried every day this week...
no response...
didn't mention cube...
Bixby quickly replied.
Keep trying...
starting solve now
see if Hucklebee
will let u launch in

Bixby knew it was easier to ask Hucklebee to let Tipton over than her dad or Arthur.

Nope...
coding assignment
due tonight b4 break
maybe l8tr?

"Zero for two," she grumbled, annoyed at the second "no," and a potential "ignore" by Marin in a matter of a few minutes. With her dad still at work for a few more hours, and her mom knee-deep in toddlers, Bixby spotted the cube on the mantle of the Great Hall where she left it for the H-bots to research while she was in school.

"Looks like it's you and me, Daryl," she said, referring to the guy who was setting off the fireworks inside the miniature scene.

Bixby had stared at it for so long, most of the mini people had been given names. During her puzzle brain breaks, she started vocally pretending they were having conversations. To anyone else, Bixby was probably going a little mad, but it helped her mind not turn to Jell-O. When Bixby left the box on the mantle this morning, Zoey, the lady dressed in purple, had just found out that Greta in green, as a prank, had given Zoey's dog a laxative in hopes that he would make a mess all over her house.

"Nobody messes with Zoey's prize dog," Bixby said before she'd launched into school earlier that morning. Now that school was over and Bixby had time to continue her make-believe scenario, tensions in the castle were high, and it would only take something small to set off a very ugly scene. That's why

Bixby could only talk to the one man who didn't care what drama was happening between the rich people inside the castle: Daryl, the lone guy hidden in the corner of the balcony.

Tomorrow she'd create a new narrative but keep their names for continuity's sake. No matter what would unfold in the next day's rendition, she was convinced Daryl would always be her favorite for some reason. But for the rest of the night, Bixby was stumped, and no book, journal, online search, visit to the library, orientation of the box, or variant of the scene produced a sliver of understanding.

The cube sat on her pillow playing the scene on a continuous loop as she slipped into the darkness of sleep with only one question on repeat.

"How do you find a castle that doesn't exist?"

CHAPTER 5

CONFIRMATION

911

The emergency text pinged on Bixby's Holo-Writer early the next morning. Between friends, it was agreed upon to never ignore a 911 text, so Bixby sat up when her Holo-Writer showed she had a video chat request.

"This had better be a real 911, Tipton," she grumbled as she cleared her eyes.

"Good morning, Sunshine," came a chipper female voice.

"Pippa?" Bixby adjusted the view of her screen so she could see and found it wasn't merely a call between her and Tipton. This was a three-way conference call.

"I thought we talked about this, Tipton," Bixby said with a frown.

Tipton, in turn, looked to Pippa. "Told you she'd be mad."

"Don't worry, Bixby. It's not his fault," Pippa said. "I hacked him. He didn't have a choice."

Bixby was too tired to doubt her assertion. It wasn't a secret at school that Pippa was tremendously gifted behind a keyboard, but between her chipper attitude and hacking her best friend, Bixby was certain Pippa needed to be kept at a distance.

"How is it possible you are happy at..." Bixby yawned and rubbed the sleep out of her eyes as she looked at the clock on her nightstand.

"Four a.m.," Pippa filled in.

Bixby didn't know exactly what time she had finally nodded off, but she was positive that she could count on one hand the hours she had slept.

"It's definitely Level Two," Tipton said out of the blue.

Bixby jerked wide awake. "How do you know?"

They both grinned mischievously into their Holo-Writers.

"You tell her," Tipton gushed.

"No, you tell her. It was your idea. I just helped a little."

"One of the two of you had better spill the beans, or I'm blocking both of you," Bixby growled.

"I hacked the Daggers," Pippa giggled. "So easy."

"Wow, you really must not like your life," Bixby said, shocked at their bold and illegal move.

"Oh man. You should've seen how she pulled it off," Tipton said. "It was nuts."

Pippa filled in the rest. "Wrote a little virus that gave me a backdoor to Penny's Holo-Writer which she had linked to an H-bot."

Bixby could care less about the technical aspect of how they did it because, frankly, she didn't understand it. All she heard was that the Daggers had an H-bot that Pippa was able to access while its system was charging.

"What does that have to do with Level Two?" Bixby asked.

"I accessed the H-bot's eyes and used them as spy cameras."

"Not creepy at all," Bixby replied.

"And I watched as Wesley's family sat around their dinner table and studied the same castle that you have, fireworks and all," she said.

"For legality's sake, I am going to pretend that I only heard the part where you know that the Daggers have the same cube as I do," Bixby replied.

"Bixby, you're going to Level Two as soon as you find out where that castle is," Tipton said. He knew how anxious not knowing made Bixby, but he couldn't imagine how bad her anxiety had peaked knowing that this was indeed Level Two.

"Which means I only have today and tomorrow to figure out where this castle is," she said with a heavy sigh.

"Oh, and Penny has hacks and spyware on all of your school devices, FYI," Pippa said, letting the other shoe drop on the situation. "So be careful what you do around them."

"Is she listening to this?" Bixby asked, ready to end the call.

"I put up a few different firewalls and called you at a ridiculous time in the morning in hopes to tell you that securely," she started. "But someone has already torn down the first firewall, so I would say she will be on to us momentarily."

"But now you know," Tipton added quickly, trying to ease the tension of letting Pippa in on the team unintentionally.

"Any last questions before she breaches the wall?" Pippa asked as she began clacking away at her computer.

"Is Tipton compromised on launching here, and how do I get ahold of you again?" Bixby asked feeling a little more confident of Pippa's intentions.

"No worries on Tipton's launch because his coin is the only one of its kind, and I'll reach out to you when it's safe," Pippa answered.

"She's through," Tipton tacked on.

Before anyone could say anything else, the call went dead.

"I guess I won't be going back to sleep now, will I Daryl?" she said plopping back down on her pillow to watch the little man set off fireworks again. "So much for Christmas break."

At that point, she pulled on a hoodie, tucked the cube under her arm, and headed to the kitchen in the hopes that Miss Marmalade would be willing to make her peanut butter pancakes, even if it was incredibly early.

Bixby didn't want to worry her family about Level Two any more than they already were, so she said nothing about her 4 a.m. video call as they trickled in the kitchen later that morning. Her mom would become more panicked, and her dad would flood her with all kinds of unsolicited advice. They usually meant well, but sometimes it was too much.

Knowing that her school equipment was compromised, Bixby pretended to let her family help by giving them opportunities to be the ones who searched out the ideas throughout the morning. She could tell that she had fooled everybody except for one: Harvey. Being that he was the house system, Harvey must have heard the early morning conversation, but neither of them had the opportunity to discuss it without prying ears. The best they could do was exchange glances, knowing that they needed to talk.

"Can you list the all the places we've thought this castle could be?" her dad asked the robots after a long while of getting nowhere.

As the list was made, Bixby turned her own thoughts over in her head. "Places it could be…" Bixby murmured slowly. "Places it could be…"

Arthur, taking note, looked up at her. "What was that?"

"Dad said places the cube could be," she replied. "What if the castle's location isn't on a map?"

"Say again?" her dad asked, still confused.

"Oh!" she cried out as her brain struck proverbial gold. "Home isn't the location of that castle!"

Bixby waited a beat for the others to catch up to her revelation, but no one did. Hucklebee even argued. "It literally says 'Find My Home.'"

"Yeah, but it's a play-on-words puzzle," she explained. "We are not looking for the home of the person who sent it, or even where the castle is, if that's the home. We're looking for the home of the cube!"

"You think the cube is a key then?" her dad asked, clearly impressed by Bixby's ability to think this puzzle through. "If so, that means there has to be a lock around here somewhere it will fit into, right?"

"Like the cube in Cody's clock?" Harvey asked.

"Precisely," Bixby said, answering both of their questions simultaneously. "Harvey, can you search the house for a place that would fit that sized cube?"

"Give me a moment," he replied before starting his scan. He knew every inch of Pinnacle Manor, which made her hopeful he'd find it fast. Sadly, that wasn't the case. "There is no place that the glass box will fit like a key in any of the areas I can see."

Everyone else exchanged understanding glances. "The library!" they shouted in unison. It was the only place they knew of that Harvey was unable to scan.

Bixby panicked a little, knowing the last time she was down there she had set off a sonic explosion. Hucklebee quenched her fears with a nod and a wink as everyone hustled through the Great Room towards the fireplace in Bixby's room.

As they burst through her bedroom door, Mr. Timmons' Holo-Watch made its all too familiar ring when he was being called into work.

"How in the world did they know I was up so early?" Mr. Timmons grumbled.

"Penny," Bixby muttered. It had to be her eavesdropping, and she told her dad, the Foreman.

Either that, or Pinnacle Manor was compromised somewhere else, too.

It all made Bixby's head spin at how devious everyone was being. She wanted the games outside of the Riddle to stop, but she kept reminding herself, *People act ridiculous for a lot of money or fame.*

"Sorry guys, I have to go in," her dad said once the call was over.

"Aww," everyone said in unison, knowing he didn't have a choice.

"We'll manage," her mom replied. "But hurry home when you can."

Her dad nodded. "You bet."

As her dad went to leave, Bixby shot in a quick request. "Can Tipton at least come over to help?"

"Normal rules apply," he said, kissing her on the head and turning back towards his room to get in his Holo-Launch Suit.

With her dad out of the picture and Miss Marmalade staying behind to watch the twins, Bixby was left short-handed, but it was better than being alone heading down to the library.

Bixby held her breath and rolled the combination lock to its open position. The gears and latches spun and clanked as the door readied itself to open. She exhaled when she saw Hucklebee had already cleaned up the mess. He had not disappointed her.

"I always love coming down to this place," Mrs. Timmons said. "Just wish we didn't have to go down so many stairs to get here. Or up, leaving."

"Alright, let's find this cube's spot," Bixby said. "It's got to be here somewhere."

A moment later, Tipton appeared, having made a successful launch inside. "I'm here!" he said. "And oh, man, it looks so much—"

Bixby shot a stern look that burned through him like laser beams.

Tipton was quick to alter the rest of his comment.

"—nicer after Hucklebee dusted."

Hucklebee could only roll his eyes and shake his head at the awful performance. Luckily for them, the rest of the team was too occupied by their search to notice. For the next few hours, everyone there set the cube in about a million locations to no avail. Something Tipton said the day prior about being in Cody's private library had Bixby more and more convinced this wasn't right as the time rolled on. It also made Bixby more and more frustrated that she couldn't figure it out.

"I think we're in the wrong place," Bixby eventually said.

Arthur tilted his head. "What do you mean? Logically, this has to be the place."

"I don't think anyone else has a secret library," Bixby replied.

Her mom looked skeptical of the claim. "How do we know that?"

"We don't, but something is off with this search," she said, crossing her arms and grinding her teeth in disappointment. The fact that the cube had a firework display with a countdown to the twenty-third flickering every thirty seconds didn't help either. She was down to what was left of today and tomorrow to solve this riddle.

"I will have to agree with Bixby's intuition; this doesn't seem right," Harvey said, rubbing the back of his hand.

Hucklebee offered a shrug. "Do you want us to continue to search for castles in the real world?"

"I'm not sure yet. I need time to think, but I'm certain this isn't it," Bixby huffed. She hunched over the wooden desk and leaned her weight on it. She was convinced she was on to something, but everything kept leading her to more and more dead ends. If this was a puzzle box *in* Level Two, she would definitely be in last place.

"How about we go back upstairs, get some food in us, let the H-bots recharge, and give our brains a little break," Mrs. Timmons suggested. Everyone nodded in agreement. "Maybe Dad will come home with a fresh idea?"

Nobody agreed with her wishful thinking but knew that Mrs. Timmons was trying to stay positive.

"Okay," Bixby said. She could feel the tension and anxiety building in her muscles, and with that, she feared her mood might not only sour her own thoughts and abilities, but her team's as well.

The group started up the stairs though Bixby lagged behind, as did Harvey.

"Do you know what is bugging me the most?" Harvey quietly asked.

"What's that?" she asked, hoping it didn't have anything to do with her nuking the library earlier.

Harvey shot a knowing grin but said nothing on that matter. "What bugs me the most is the feeling that there was something not right in Level One," he said. "I've watched the video and analyzed it at least a million times, and I cannot for the life of me figure out what is off about it, but I know there's something."

"Wait, you're not mad about the library?" Bixby asked, thinking he was trying to get the truth about the sonic boom to finally come out.

"What was wrong with the library?" he replied back almost sarcastically which wasn't his normal approach to their conversations.

"You're not mad I blew it up?" she admitted.

"Did you now?" he replied with a straight face. "Strange. Hucklebee didn't say anything about it in his daily uploads. Clearly then, you're exaggerating the mess. I'm sure it was something, but I doubt it was catastrophic."

"No, Harvey, I—"

"I see no mess," he said, cutting her off. "No harm. No foul. Right? Even if you *did* do something…horrible… I see no reason to dwell when the damage done is no more. There are more important things to attend to, correct?"

Bixby nodded, grateful for the grace he was extending. No doubt, he could see she was at wit's end already.

"I'm struggling a lot, Harvey," she confessed. "Ever since I found my way into this riddle, everyone seems to want to be part of the solution."

Harvey looked at her, confused. "People wanting to help is a bad thing?"

"Having everyone take part in the solving of this puzzle box is too chaotic and makes me feel out of control," she replied. "Too many chefs in the kitchen, you know? And now I have to worry about new people taking part, people I don't know I can trust, and the deadline is almost here, and…and…and I just can't think straight anymore."

"That does seem like a lot to handle," he said.

"Yeah," she said. "I just feel like I solve puzzles better when I'm alone."

"You really don't want anyone's help?" he asked.

It took Bixby a moment to consider the thought before she spoke. "Since this whole riddle started, Dad is constantly being pulled into work, and I can't help but to think that it's partially my fault. Then there are the rules where Tipton can only be here during visiting hours, and now he is letting Pippa help, which I don't like at all. Mom is always with the boys. Miss Marmalade is keeping this place running with Arthur, who wants no part of this usually. Today was the first day I didn't have Penny chattering in my ear…" she paused only briefly for a quick breath before finishing her rant, "...and you haven't been around for a while," Bixby said, completing her list of annoyances. The last part was hard to say, but Bixby was reaching the end of her rope. "It's all a mess."

"How long have you been feeling like this?" he asked as they approached the top of the staircase.

Bixby slowed her pace up to think.

"It doesn't matter," she finally said. "It's what it is now. The more people who get involved the more I feel like I'm either failing them, or I'm losing control. Or both. In the end, I need to do this alone." When Harvey didn't say anything for a few seconds, Bixby filled in the silence. "Plus, I can't let Level One be a fluke because the other teams will take advantage of that if I'm relying on everyone else to help me win."

"Nonsense," Harvey replied sternly. "As I have said before, I've watched the first level a million times. They're terrified of your abilities," he said. "And rightfully so, I might add. Besides, no champion in any sport or contest throughout all of history has become the victor solely on their own abilities."

"Maybe, but this riddle," she said as she held up the plexiglass box, "isn't making me very confident of anything right now."

At this point, they'd reached and pushed their way through the fireplace entrance. Bixby slumped down on the end of her bed with the cube placed beside her, the golden evening light from a setting sun casting warmly across it.

As Bixby stayed on her bed, Harvey made his way to the door and turned with one final thought.

"I do not believe the Riddle was meant to boost your confidence Bixby," he said. "I think it was meant to test your resolve."

Chapter 6
A Closer Look

As the fireplace roared in front of her, Bixby sat in her egg chair staring aimlessly into the dancing flame. She hadn't left her room since the group had come back upstairs to rest. Oblivious to what time it was, she only knew it was past bedtime. She felt lost, and even sleep couldn't overtake her doubting thoughts. Could she really do any of this?

Secretly, she hoped her dad would come home to help calm her nerves. It was to no avail. The Daggers knew the game was afoot, so the Foreman undoubtedly was keeping him from helping, which soured her even more.

Bixby was still convinced that this was a puzzle similar to the one Cody had given her with his clock when the challenge first started so long ago. Occasionally, she looked at it sitting on her nightstand with digital fish swimming to-and-fro. But this time, the key had no keyhole. What was she missing? Her stomach let her know that the one thing she was indeed missing was food. She slid on her house slippers and crept her way down to the kitchen. There she built a monster turkey, cheese, and hot sauce sandwich. Daryl and the scene took his usual place in front of her as she chomped away.

"Come on D... give me a hint," she whispered with her chin on the table as she chewed, making her head bobble around with every bite.

He didn't give her one.

"Fine, have it your way, but if I don't make it there to see you, don't be mad at me," she muttered.

Still nothing.

"Don't worry; I'll be mad at me enough for the both of us," she sighed. She then practically pressed her face against the glass so that she could see every pixel of the fireworks. Each letter was a different pristine color.

"I wish I was there already," Bixby said, hoping that all she had to do was wish to make it true.

Wait... I can't do that, but what if I projected myself there? she wondered.

Bixby decided not to grab her Holo-Suit because she was only going to have her launch room magnify the cube to life sized.

Punching a few buttons outside of her Launch Room, Bixby pulled up the sequence that she wanted the computer to perform.

Before stepping into her room, she checked her dad's panel: he was still hunkered behind a desk, frantically trying to make something work on his screen. She loved him to the moon and back, but the Riddle made him miss so much time with her. It was a no-win situation in her mind and why she didn't hold a grudge against him. It wasn't his fault he wasn't around, but it was still extremely frustrating.

Bixby placed her cube in the center of the room. As the first light entered the space, she closed her eyes and let the light bounce off the walls, building the image she programmed the computers to run.

The scene inside the cube suddenly grew so it filled the whole space around her, and Bixby found herself on the balcony near Daryl, gazing up at the fireworks. While they were fun to watch, what caught her eye were the people inside the castle, mingling in a ballroom. Each one of them was magnificently dressed in an array of colorful gowns, their faces all covered in headgear to hide their identity. Though she already knew that it was a masquerade ball, to see it up close was mesmerizing. From the outside window, she searched the room, but found no clue, puzzle, or riddle to solve. As such, she chose to move on to another part of the castle.

She had the program move her into the ballroom among the holographic people, but that turned out to be a bust as well.

Next, she went out on the front lawn and watched the drama unfold between Zoey and Greta. Bixby's fake drama between them wasn't as exciting when the two ladies were life-sized and their mouths didn't move, but Bixby imagined the conflict again anyway.

After watching it a few times through, she searched the front lawn for any clue as to where the cube's home was or how to find it. Yet again, her search led to a dead end, but she thought that she would invite everyone to join her there tomorrow and take a crack at finding something.

For now, her body was telling her that she had better shut it down or she was going to be exhausted later that morning. Before she unlaunched, she jumped back to the balcony where the fireworks were life-sized and spectacular from below. She could barely tell they were spelling letters, because from her perspective now they were massive explosions.

"Daryl, I'd say outstanding show if it weren't for the bottom of that firework being the wrong color," Bixby said. The moment those words left her mouth, a shiver went up her spine as a new thought dawned on her. "Wait, Cody doesn't miscode anything."

Bixby searched the program to bring something up for her.

"Launch any other scan Harvey took of the cube and keep me in the same spot," she instructed.

The Launch Room made the adjustment and Bixby gasped: the discoloration of the fireworks was no longer there.

"Show me another scan. Same parameters," Bixby said.

One pixel was now red instead of blue.

"Program. Where was the first scan taken?"

Letters printed out in front of her:

Bedroom: Bixby Timmons

"Program. Where was the second scan taken?"

Letters again printed out in front of her:

Great Hall

"Switch to the live cube shot," she commanded.

Daryl robotically turned to light the fireworks. They took off into the night sky, exploding like the million other times she had watched it. Except this time, the four pixels at the base of the letter 'F' at the beginning of the sentence were not blue, but red instead.

"Clever," Bixby whispered.

She raced out of the Launch Room and right into Arthur's chest.

"Sorry," she yelped as she stumbled backwards.

"It is way past bedtime, Bixby," Arthur scolded.

"I know, but I couldn't sleep, and I think I'm on to something," she replied.

"Do tell."

With that, she hurried back to her room with Arthur in tow.

"Scan the fireworks and tell me if any pixels are the wrong color," she said as she pulled her favorite sweatshirt.

"The invitation seems to be in order," he replied after his scan.

"Great, now follow me," she said, already making her way out the door. Once they traveled to and stopped in the middle of the Great Room, she turned to face him. "Scan again."

"There's a wrong pixel now," he said. "It's at the base of the letter 'F' in 'find,'" he said.

Bixby clapped her hands together. "Perfect. Let's go!"

Arthur followed her to the kitchen, grumbling a bit. When she got there, she asked the same, and he reported that three pixels were now a different color.

"What's this all about?" Arthur asked.

"I think we are playing *Hotter or Colder*," Bixby said, grinning from ear to ear.

"My scan of this game tells me that it is rather easy to play," he replied.

Bixby and Arthur continued down the corridor, and, true to form, the pixels continued to change from blue to red.

"I know you say it is not okay to go outside this late at night, but it's the logical next step," Bixby said standing at the door that had "To The Lighthouse" written above it.

"I'll summon your parents," Arthur said. "I'm certain they'll want to be a part of this."

"Great. You do that, and I'll follow the cube," she replied. With that, she dashed through the door into the crisp air outside.

Arthur immediately gave chase. "Wait!"

"I thought you were getting my parents!" she called back. She could have stopped, but her determination wouldn't let her slow down during the chase for answers. The pixels were changing faster and faster, and, deep down, she wanted to solve this part on her own for her sake.

"I sent a memo to Harvey to do it!" he shouted back, trying to keep up.

Bixby reached the bottom of the stairs and dashed out onto the beach, running towards the water as that's where she assumed the game was leading her.

Bixby skidded to a stop as a pixel turned back to blue.

"Colder," she whispered to herself as she turned back around towards the lighthouse that sat tucked into the rockface above the dunes.

"Colder," she grumbled again when the path up to the lighthouse wasn't correct. The game ultimately ran Bixby right up against a large rock wall.

"What do we do now?" Arthur asked. "Climbing this wall will only lead us back to Pinnacle Manor."

"I don't think we're supposed to go up," she said, putting the cube in her hoodie pocket.

In front of her was a well-carved-out ledge. On the ledge were five fairly round stones. Bixby picked the first one up and turned it over in her hand. It was smooth as if it had sat in a river for hundreds of years being polished.

"Yellow," she said grabbing the next stone. It too was perfectly smooth.

"Green," she said, examining the one after in the moonlight.

Each stone was shaped the same but had a slightly different tint. Bixby didn't need to pull the cube from her pocket as she returned the stones to their locations in a specific color pattern.

"How do you know which one goes where?" Arthur inquired.

"The first letter in each word of the fireworks riddle is capitalized, and also shaded in one of these five stones' color," Bixby said, placing the third rock in its place.

From how rigid Arthur became, she knew that he had pulled up a scan of the cube and was confirming her hypothesis.

"I believe you're correct," he said, sounding impressed.

She smiled and placed the red stone in its new home. The five rocks were now in order, and a small trap door opened under each one and swallowed them whole. The weight of each of the rocks must have hit a pad correctly and clacking like the library door opening up could be heard.

"A weighted lock," Bixby said, excited at her newfound success.

"Care to explain?"

"Each rock has a specific weight, but close enough to each other that it would be difficult if not impossible to tell apart by hand. Each pad is calibrated to not unlock unless the correct weight is put on that pad. So, when I put all the right rocks on all the right scales, it triggered the locking mechanism to open," she replied.

"In essence, it's a digital lock that is looking for the scale to read the right weight in the right order?"

"Exactly," she said as she peered into the open rock wall door.

Lights clicked on as she stepped on the metal landing just inside the threshold. To her surprise, the stairs there were similar to the ones that led down to the library.

With that, Bixby flew down them, grinning from ear to ear.

CHAPTER 7
SELECTIVE HEARING

"We should wait for your parents to get here," Arthur called out from behind.

"They can catch up!" Bixby shouted, pushing harder down to the bottom of the stairs, and skidding to a halt on the wet concrete floor. She peered into the cube, and the letter "F" was now almost completely red.

"We've got to be getting close," she said. Above her were large pipes and conduits all painted the same color as the walls and floors. "Any guesses as to where this all leads?"

Arthur scanned it all. "None of this is used for Pinnacle Manor; it is all foreign to me."

From high above them, they could hear footsteps.

"See?" Bixby asked. "They're coming."

The two pressed onward, and each time they got to the edge of whatever light was available, more lights would turn on and illuminate the next section they had to go through. Heart racing, anticipation surging through her system, Bixby broke into a full sprint.

"Strange I never knew about this place," Arthur said as they went.

"Yeah, well, this makes the second secret area Cody has kept from his programs and H-bots," she replied.

The last light to come on illuminated a seamless concrete wall; it was a dead end except for the small square pad in the very middle of the massive barrier.

"Now what?" Arthur asked.

"Two pixels left to turn red," Bixby said as she approached the wall. She held the cube up to the pad like a key fob.

BLEEP

"Access granted," said a synthesized voice that came from keypad.

The ground rumbled, and Bixby instinctively took a few steps back. What looked like a concrete wall was in fact an encased steel door that was retracting into the side wall as sirens rang out.

"No way!" she exclaimed, eyes wide. Quickly, she stepped over the threshold and looked down at the ten wide, descending steps that greeted her. Those stairs ended at the water's edge, and inside the giant room, perched in the water, sat a huge floating secret.

"A hidden submarine bay," Arthur gasped.

Before he could reach down and hold her back, Bixby was skipping every other step on the way to the landing and a plank that was attached to the underwater monster.

"Get back here this instant!" he barked as her feet hit the plank with a rattle of metal on metal.

"What did you say?" she shouted back, still going.

"Don't you dare climb that ladder, young lady," he said, racing after her.

It was no use; this was way too cool for Arthur to stop her when she was so close to an answer. He would have had an easier time getting a rattlesnake to let him scratch its belly.

"At least try not to touch anything until your parents get here!" he pleaded.

The hatch into the sub was wide open. She stuffed the cube into her hoodie pocket, and, using the trick she learned on the library ladder, grabbed the handles, and slid down inside the belly of the beast.

The sound inside the ship hummed and churned like a symphony of unwanted instruments playing in harmony. There was only one narrow hallway that led to, what she could only assume, the entire length of the ship. There were hatch doors on either side of the ship that could hold anything, but Bixby knew where she had to go. There was an open area not more than twenty feet from where she stood, and it was glowing red.

Upon exploration, it was the control center of the submarine. She had seen enough ship movies to recognize the bridge: both boat and starship bridges always seemed to look relatively the same to her.

"Captain's chair," she said while climbing up past the rails where the sub's workers would sit and do their tasks.

"Stop right there, Miss Timmons!" Arthur yelped, finally catching up to her.

Bixby dropped in the chair and spun it around a few times. "Isn't this the most amazing thing you have ever seen?"

"No further until everyone gets here," he begged.

"No further," she agreed.

A few moments passed, and Bixby ended up looking down at the cube that had one pixel left blinking blue. She was near to the answer, and it felt good to be zeroed in on the solution, but the temptation to not do *something* else was killing her.

"Arthur!" the familiar sound of Harvey rang through the hull of the ship.

"Down here," Arthur called back. Bixby could almost immediately hear him groan down every rung as he climbed aboard.

"Welcome to the party," Bixby said. Once he reached the bridge, she looked at him, perplexed. "Where's everyone else?"

"I was able to get into my Holo-Body at the base of the rock wall before venturing down to yet another area of Pinnacle Manor that I have no data on," he replied, sounding annoyed. "The rest of the group had just gathered in the Great Hall when I made my way down."

"Man, it's going to take them forever to get here then," she replied with a huff while rolling the cube in her hands a few times. "We should check out the rest of the sub then while we wait. Make sure there are no surprises."

"Not on our life," Harvey said. "Sit there and wait."

Bixby groaned. "Fine, whatever," she said plopping the cube on the chair next to her with a click. Her eyes drifted down to the chair's arm where the cube rested securely inside a divot.

Find my home, she immediately thought.

"Whoops," she said, knowing she had unintentionally finished the solve, but not sad that it had happened either.

Instantaneously, lights and sirens started to ring through the air, and the squeal of the hatch door closing pierced the inside of the bridge.

"Now what have you done?" Arthur said.

"All I did was put the cube down!" she shot back. "It's not like I hit a bunch of buttons or anything!"

"You were supposed to wait! That was the deal!" Arthur shouted above the wailing of the ship.

"I was!" she yelled back over the noise.

The floor beneath her shifted, and she could feel the sub moving forward. Not only moving forward, but descending beneath the water, too.

"Oh, no! It's leaving!" she shouted. Panick ripped through her soul as she raced out of the bridge, desperate to try and get to the outer hatch before it was too late. She didn't have anything she needed for Level Two, and she didn't get to say goodbye to her family.

A metal squeal told her that she didn't make it in time. Not by a long shot. Reaching the base of the ladder, she could see the hatch above was already tightly locked and sealed. Even seeing that, Bixby raced up the ladder, tears stinging her cheeks, and tried the wheel to get it open.

It didn't budge.

"Come on. Open," she groaned over and over as her muscles strained against the intense demand she set upon them. "Open up! Open up! Open up!"

"Bixby!" Harvey's sharp bellow stopped her in her place. "You can't open it anymore."

"Maybe if we—"

"No, he means you mustn't," Arthur clarified. "We're underwater. You'll flood the sub and kill all both."

Bixby swallowed hard at the implications of what was going on but was far from defeated. She slid back down the ladder, nearly flooring Harvey in the process, and raced back to the bridge.

Once there, she tried pulling the miniature castle from its resting spot. "It won't budge either," she said.

Harvey's attention was elsewhere. "I believe we're leaving Worthy Lake."

"Are you sure?" Arthur asked.

"Quite. My signal is weakening with every passing moment. I cannot project into my Holo-Body outside of a certain range of Pinnacle Manor," he explained. "I suspect it won't be long before I disappear from the sub."

"You can't leave me to babysit," Arthur protested.

Bixby, now coming to terms with the fact that what was unfolding was not something she could stop, sprang into action, wanting to give her parents something they could hold onto.

"Harvey, I need you to record this message for my family," Bixby said, standing directly in front of Harvey.

"Recording now," he replied with a short nod.

"Dad. Mom. I'm sorry I pushed ahead, but I honestly didn't mean to launch this sub! Please know that I will do my best to be safe. I'm not sure if I will be able to communicate with you inside the Riddle, but if there is a way, I will find it. I love—"

Then Harvey was gone.

Bixby and Arthur stared at each other for several moments before Arthur finally broke the silence. "Where is this thing taking us?"

Bixby turned and pointed to the cube, specifically the little man on the balcony setting off fireworks. "We're going to visit Daryl."

CHAPTER 8
THE REAL TIPTON ELLERBY

Bixby explored the sub, starting from the bow and working her way aft. Most of the inner hatch doors were locked with important signs emblazoned on the door like "Electrical Room," or "Pump Room." Since this was a sub, it was probably a good idea to lock those hatches and not let her snoop around for fear her clumsiness would end up sending them permanently to Davey Jones' locker. Either way, Bixby had to make sure that the ship wasn't the next part of the puzzle.

Am I on my way to Level Two or is this like the limo in Level One and we've already begun? she thought to herself as she went.

The one hatch that did open was labeled, "Crew's Mess & Galley." It was a fairly tidy eating space and kitchen, which made her wonder why it was called a "Mess," but she didn't waste time pondering it for long.

"Nothing," she informed Arthur on her way back through the bridge. She could see that he was busy pecking away at controls around the ship to see if he could get anything to react to his frantic button mashing.

"I strongly despise autopilot," he growled.

"Any idea where in the world we are?" Bixby asked.

Arthur plopped into the captain's chair with a huff. "That also is a mystery."

"Can you tell if this ship is a Launch Room, and we are simply floating around Worthy Lake?" she asked.

"I do not find that to be a likely scenario given that Harvey's signal faded out of range," he said confidently. "And for this to be a Launch Room, you would need a Holo-Suit. You, Miss Timmons, have not changed that sweatshirt in at least two days."

Looking down at her favorite hoodie, Bixby realized he wasn't wrong, so she changed the subject. "Well, I'm going to check out the rest of this place to make sure it's not part of the riddle."

Bixby went back to exploring, still heading aft. More locked hatch doors greeted her until the final two.

The first door was labeled, "Sleeping Quarters," with Bixby's name on a scratch pad underneath it. There was, however, no door handle or latch for her to unhook. Bixby placed her fingers and thumb on the scratch pad to no avail.

"Arthur?" Bixby cried out, hoping he could hear her.

"How may I assist you, Bixby?" Arthur asked as he made his way from the bridge down the hall.

"I think I found our rooms," she started. "But I can't figure out how to open them."

After a few moments of inspecting her door and the hinges, Arthur was stumped, so he proceeded to the next door and began playing with the scratch pad.

"This one is not for me," he said, stepping away from the door.

"But we're the only two in the ship," she replied.

"I understand that, but when I scratch my name on the unmarked pad, it says, 'Invalid Assistant. No H-Bots allowed.'"

Bixby's face scrunched. "Invalid Assistant?" she repeated. "Does that mean I get someone to help me with this Level?"

"I would say it does, but it looks like I'm not that someone," Arthur replied with a huff. "Maybe you should have waited for your family, and you would have more people on the ship to choose from?"

Bixby clenched her jaw, annoyed at his tone and how right he was. She wondered if it was worth a try to see if she could get the ship to turn around, so she took her place in front of the second pad. There was a really smart guy who loved riddles just as much as she did, and she really wanted him to be there with her. He had helped her a lot in the first riddle and would be invaluable as an assistant in Level Two. Reaching up, she scratched his name on the pad.

DAD

She knew it was a longshot, but he was who she really wanted to do this riddle with.

The screen began to flash:

Invalid Assistant

"Oh, come on, Cody," Bixby groaned, rolling her eyes. She crossed her arms over her chest and drummed her fingers as she thought things through for a bit. "What if I have to pick who I have to compete against first or share the sub with?" she eventually said.

"If it is who you have to compete against, I would pick Greg. But if it is who you have to share the ship with, it would be Marin," Arthur suggested.

"But if I pick Marin, and it is who I need to compete with, then one of us eliminates the other," the decision was starting to make her anxious.

"I think Greg is the safest bet either way; he isn't a huge threat to your intelligence, and Marin could most certainly beat Wesley," Arthur pointed out.

Bixby still didn't like any of it. "Okay, but what if it's neither?"

"I'm not sure I understand what you're getting at."

"Cody isn't going to let one person pick everyone's roommate or competition," she confidently said, reaching up to the pad. "He's letting me pick someone to stay on the ship and help me navigate the masquerade ball."

"Let's be honest, you really only have one friend, and, luckily for you, he knows a little bit about computers," Arthur said with his usual bluntness.

"I'm well aware of that fact Arthur, but thank you for pointing that out," she replied. "But if Tipton is allowed to Holo-Coin in and help me, he could also patch in my family which would be awesome."

With that, Bixby reached up and scribbled out his name:

TIPTON ELLERBY

The normal response of "Invalid Assistant" did not flash up this time. In its place read:

APPROVED

Bixby and Arthur both slammed shoulder-first into the hull next to them, and then to the floor as the sub made a sharp right turn.

"What on earth?" Bixby shouted as she tried to find her footing.

"Trying to figure that out now," Arthur replied, stumbling his way to the bridge.

Bixby followed.

When they got there, they saw a map of the world that had now popped up on the navigation desk with a pinging noise ringing out every few rotations of the sonar line.

"It would appear that we are headed for that tiny little town off the coast of Maine," he said pointing to a glowing blip on the map.

Bixby grinned. "Tipton lives in Maine."

"The real Tipton?"

"The real Tipton," Bixby answered.

Arthur sighed heavily. "It wasn't enough that I have to babysit you, but now we are on our way to pick up the real Tipton Ellerby."

Bixby smiled a little at his agony. The thought of having someone here on the sub helping her navigate the riddle was a bit thrilling. Maybe having Arthur there was an added bonus. If that were true, Cody had really outdone himself this time.

"I hope they have a junk yard where we're going, because I'm ready to throw myself in the compacter," he groaned.

"Oh, stop that. He's not that bad," she said, making herself comfortable in the First-Mate's chair.

"I'd rather have my memory chips resoldered with acid than listen to him talk to that girlfriend of his."

Bixby could only chuckle because she didn't know who annoyed her more with their pet name-calling: Tipton and Pippa, or her parents. Either way, it was still unpleasant to hear, and it apparently unnerved Arthur also as his robotic face soured at the sound of it.

"How long until we get there?" Bixby asked.

Quickly computing how fast their dot was approaching Tipton's dot, Arthur answered, "Three hours."

"Then I'm headed to the mess hall to see if I can make a sandwich."

* * *

Arthur's timing on the sub was near to the minute as the sound of groaning metal bellowed throughout the sub. Bixby could tell they were slowing down, and her feet nearly left the ground as the sub bobbed up and settled back down. She could only guess that they were now out of the water. Her suspicions were quickly confirmed by the screeching of the hatch that she had hastily climbed down a short while earlier.

"I'll go first to make sure it is safe," Arthur said sternly as he reached for the rails to ascend.

77

Bixby, still not learning her lesson of patience, was on his heels and they reached the platform within moments of each other. He rolled his eyes at her inability to follow rules very well.

"This could be the next step in Level Two," she said.

"I do wonder why I bother," he grumbled as the two of them scanned their location.

They were in the middle of what looked like another lake, but, as she turned, she could see the harbor let out into the endless ocean.

"There doesn't seem to be anyone here," she said.

"I'm not that lucky," Arthur replied, pointing to a small fishing vessel that came around the river bend and headed for them.

Out on the very front of the boat was the unmistakable Tipton Ellerby. He was standing on the rail waving as frantically as he could. So much so that the boat captain leaned out of his window and shouted something to him. Bixby could only imagine it was the man telling Tipton to get off the rail that he was most definitely going to fall off of as he continued to wave.

"I am secretly hoping that boat hits a rock and sinks," Arthur confessed.

"Try to be nice for once," she said, climbing down the ladder. "He's not that bad. You might end up liking him."

In no time, Tipton was ready to board Bixby's newly acquired ship.

"Thank you!" Tipton shouted to the captain as he bounded down the plank and onto the sub. He then eyed the whole thing. "Man, where did you get this?"

"Found it hidden at Pinnacle Manor," she explained.

"Are you parents down below then?" he asked.

Bixby shook her head. "No."

"No?"

"No," she repeated. "They're back home. What makes you think they'd be here?"

"I got a message from Harvey that said I was invited to a Timmons surprise Christmas party and instructions on how to get here," he said, hitching a thumb toward the ship that brought him in.

Arthur chuckled. "Nobody ever taught you about 'stranger danger' have they?"

Tipton's face curdled as it became clear he'd started to truly understand what could've happened by running off with some creepy old guy on a boat. "So... this isn't a Timmons Christmas party?"

Bixby shook her head.

"Does this mean you found the cube's home?"

She nodded.

"Which means Cody set all this up?"

She nodded again. "I think I selected you to help me navigate Level Two, which is why you're here in person."

"If you think you can handle it, that is," Arthur said, trying to test Tipton's resolve.

Tipton nervously bit his lip, took a deep breath in, and put out his hand to shake Bixby's.

"Hello, I'm Tipton Ellerby," he proudly proclaimed.

Bixby looked at his outstretched arm like a confused puppy, with her head tilted slightly and face awash with bewilderment. "Um. What are you doing? I know who you are."

"Yeah, I know we've been friends for a while now, but this is the first time we've met in person," he said, beaming through a goofy grin.

Bixby smiled and enjoyed the formal greeting they'd previously never had. She reached her hand out to meet his, "It's a pleasure to meet you, Tipton. My name is Bixby Timmons. Would you care to solve a riddle with me?"

"Oh brother," Arthur huffed.

Tipton tightened his grip. "Definitely."

"Don't forget to tell him that there is no way for him to call his girlfriend," Arthur prodded.

Right as he finished those words, Tipton's eyes lit up, and he let go of Bixby's hand in order to rummage through his pack and whip out a poorly wrapped gift box. "I've got something for you," he said. "I was going to give it to you at the Christmas party, but since there isn't one, and I bet they'd be useful anyhow, well...here you go."

Bixby took the gift and carefully unwrapped it. Inside was something that anyone who knew anything about anything trendy would instantly recognize.

"Tipton! Are these..." She was rendered speechless at the iconic rainbow-colored earring box.

"I may have made some modifications," he said.

Bixby opened the lid and gasped. "These are the most beautiful earrings I have ever seen."

"Your parents helped me get them," he replied, blushing a little at her praise. "Like I said, I upgraded them a bit so they'd be helpful if you got launched into something crazy like a new riddle."

The earrings in question weren't just any earrings; they were Tako earrings. Back before style had changed, people would get their ears pierced a hundred different times in all parts of their ears and cartilage. Finally, Mariam Tako designed a digital earring that would fit around the ear and clasp only once in the lobe of the ear to hold it in place. Using Pedrodian's digital shifting technology, the earrings could change color, texture, and even how many piercings it looked like you had.

Tako and Pedrodian technology had revolutionized the accessory world. People could scheme their earpiece to have any kind of artistic design imaginable and change their style without having to get pierced again. Bixby's Takos, however, were different than any of the ones she had ever seen. Hers started at her ear lobe, went all the way around the edge of her ear and had a small earbud that was embossed with the Timmons' crest that would rest snuggly inside her ear canal.

"Everyone pitched in to make them based on one of Mariam Tako's original designs," Tipton said. "Harvey revamped the family crest to fit into the design. Then Hucklebee cast them in Padrodian metal, which allowed me to use the same technology that Pedrodian suits were made of to make the earrings change colors based upon the outfit you wore. Your mother and Miss Marmalade set the program that will adjust the earrings' style and color; I have no fashion sense, so they handled all of that. Lastly, Pippa and I installed the chip we created into the earpieces that will act as an earbud, microphone, and launch coin. Everything is hidden in plain sight."

Bixby turned an earring in her hand as Tipton explained all the decadent details. She could only shake her head in disbelief.

"I think it's important to also tell you that I may have helped Pippa connect them to an unused Dragonthorp Inc. satellite, and they can call anyone you want right now." He smiled ear to ear.

At first, all the talk about how much Pippa was helping made Bixby want to stop and scold Tipton for how much he was letting her participate, but then something hit her that made her forget the growing irritation she was feeling. "Wait. I can call home?"

"Yep."

Bixby hurried to get them fitted to her ear.

"If we are connected to a Dragonthorp Inc. satellite, won't they have access to our communications?" she asked.

"Not if you put me in charge of the hack to get in," a voice soothingly replied in her ear.

"Pippa?" Bixby was uneasy to hear her voice on the other end because the team was quickly growing more crowded again.

"We set them up so that if you were to put them in and switch them on, I'd get a ping to let me know. I wanted to be able to wish you a Merry Christmas, Bixby," she said. "And how's the family shindig?"

"Well, Tipton got on a boat with a complete stranger, to go to a party that didn't exist and, luckily, we were the ones here to greet him," Bixby said.

"What? I thought it was a legit invite," he said, shrugging.

"He didn't back trace the email to confirm?" Pippa asked in disbelief. "Geez, what a rookie."

Bixby laughed and looked at Tipton to fill him in. "She called you a rookie hacker."

"Anyway," Pippa said. "Does this mean this is Level Two? And more important, does this mean I get to help?"

"I'll consider it," Bixby replied, a little put off that the girl had practically self-invited her way onto the team. "But if you wanted to help me right here and now, I need to get a call through to home."

"On it," Pippa said tapping away at a keyboard.

Bixby anxiously stood on the upper platform of the boat waiting for the earrings to ring through to Pinnacle Manor. Arthur nudged Tipton to climb down into the boat to give her time to explain to her parents what had happened. The view was breathtaking and real. It was a word that had become more blurred during her time with fancy Launch Rooms and Holo-Suits: real. Things around her smelled crisp and fresh. She could feel the cool breeze and slight mist on her cheeks. The water amplified as it hit the outer shell of the sub. Bixby hadn't noticed the subtle difference that she very easily missed in the day-to-day launches into Holo. She held tight to moments like this because real seemed hard to come by these days.

Her mom came through the line first. "Bixby!"

Bixby leapt with excitement. "Mom! It's so good to hear your voice!"

"Where are you? Harvey gave us your message. What's this about a submarine?" she asked.

"I'm, umm, not totally—"

Her dad jumped in and cut her off. "Are you okay, Bix?"

After that, it was rapid-fire questioning that she didn't have a prayer of keeping up with. Eventually, she knew she had to take charge of it all.

"Mom! Dad! I'm sorry!" she shouted. Once the line quieted, Bixby continued in a more even, calm manner. "Look, I was chasing after a hunch that turned out to be right. I promise that Arthur and I were going to wait for you to come down to the sub, but I accidentally set the cube in the place that it needed to be to turn on the engines, and then everything was a whirlwind after that."

"Oh, Bixby, why do you have to go and chase down every hairbrained idea you have alone?" Mrs. Timmons said with a heavy sigh. "Would it kill you to slow down and think every once and a while?"

The words punched Bixby in the gut. "Mom, I didn't mean to..."

"Let's everyone calm—" Mr. Timmons started and then glitched out.

"Hold on Bixby; the signal is getting bad," Pippa jumped in.

Bixby took that moment to calm herself down.

"... Bixby?" Mr. Timmons finished.

"I'm sorry I'm always messing up," Bixby said. "Honest."

"Bixby, that's not what I meant," her mother said firmly before her dad jumped in.

"We know, Bixby; we're just scared for you," Mr. Timmons said. "But we also need you to know that we are so very—"

Everything stopped. Again.

"I'm sorry, Bixby. That's it. The transmission is gone," Pippa said.

"Can you get it back?" Bixby asked. She pressed against the ship's rail hoping somehow that would get her dad back.

"I'll work on it and let you know as soon as I reconnect," Pippa said.

Bixby always cherished when her dad said things like, 'I love you,' or 'I'm proud of you.' But maybe this time he was going to say, 'frustrated,' or say that he was 'disappointed' in her pushing forward.

Deep down, she was ninety-nine percent sure what he was going to say would lift her spirits, but she desperately needed to hear him say it. That one percent of doubt was starting to kill her. Short lived was her thoughts as reality snapped her back from the mess of emotions that were piling up in her head.

"Bixby!" a shout came from below.

Bixby jumped, leaned over the railing, and looked down the ladder to see Tipton at the bottom. "Yes?"

"Better get down here; there is a new riddle," he said through a forced smile.

Bixby hesitated, wanting to talk to her parents at least for a minute more if possible.

"Can you get them back?" she asked into her Takos.

"I'll let you know as soon as I get a secure line," Pippa said.

"Tell Cody I'm coming," Bixby shouted into the depths below. She then grabbed the rails and, once again, slid down to get to work.

CHAPTER 9
CHOICES

Inside the bridge, Arthur and Tipton stood around the hologram being projected from the navigation table.

"What do we have?" Bixby asked as she approached.

"A map of the world with a bunch of random numbers underneath," Tipton said as he pointed at the long series of digits.

"Latitude and longitude," Bixby guessed.

"There are degrees, minutes, and seconds in latitude and longitude; these have none of those," Arthur said.

"We're in a submarine, in front of a globe, and most likely the right number of digits to make latitude and longitude," Bixby pointed out. "We only need to figure out where those digits point."

Tipton raised his eyebrows and shrugged at Arthur, and neither one of them objected.

"There are four highlighted points on the map," Bixby observed reaching up and trying to use her hand to digitally rotate the globe. The projection moved as she spun the world, and the numbers below the globe started changing.

"I think we have to choose which one of these four places to send the sub," Bixby continued. She was talking out loud like she normally would during a puzzle solve even though it looked like she was communicating. It was simply part of her process.

"How do we know which one to pick?" Tipton asked. Bixby continued to focus without giving a reply. Tipton knew that look very well from all the experiments in the library; Bixby was focused and didn't like being interrupted.

The trio spent the next thirty minutes trying to figure out what to do. Each was careful not to touch any of the highlighted locations, so they didn't accidentally send themselves someplace they didn't want to go.

"I wish we could push them all at the same time," Tipton lamented.

"That is not a bad idea," Bixby agreed, sitting up from the First Mate's chair that she was occupying while Arthur took his turn rotating the globe.

"I was being sarcastic. So, why is that a good idea?" Tipton asked.

"If we push them at the same time, we will be able to see what it does without giving the sub a direction to go," she theorized.

"Do you see any other option?" Arthur asked.

"I think the timer has started, and if we get it wrong, we fall behind," Bixby replied positioning herself near two of the green button-like dots on the globe.

Tipton smirked. "Or you get a burn like you did in the last riddle."

"Always there to make sure I don't forget things like that," Bixby replied, grimacing at the memory. She then reached up and turned on her Takos. "Pippa, you there?"

"Ready and waiting," she replied.

"Then you might as well be useful," Bixby said as she motioned Arthur to take the top button near Russia, and Tipton to take the lower button hovering over Australia. Bixby stood by the two buttons that were close together. "When we feed you a location in the world, you tell us information about castles in each place."

"On it," Pippa replied.

"You guys ready?" she asked as both her ship companions nodded back.

"On the count of three," she instructed as Tipton took a deep breath in.

"One, two, three, push, right?" Tipton clarified.

"Correct," Bixby said. "One, two, three, push!"

The buttons did what Bixby thought they might. With each of them pushed, the map gave information about each of the locations selected.

"Mine is Queensland, Australia," Tipton said from his side of the globe.

"Pippa. How big is Queensland?" Bixby asked.

"It's like the second largest state in Australia," she said after a few seconds of clacking at her keyboard.

"How many castles are there in Queensland?" Bixby asked. More clacking.

"There are a few real ones, and a bunch of touristy ones," Pippa relayed.

Bixby turned to Arthur. "Where's yours?"

"Moscow, Russia," he replied.

"Any of the castles there resemble the one in the cube from your searches?"

Arthur took a few seconds to finish scanning his memory. "I'm sorry, no."

"I'm over Scotland which I'm positive has a ton of castles, and I also have a place called…" Bixby paused.

"What is it?" Tipton asked.

"I've never heard of this island," Bixby said as she read some of its details.

"What is it so Pippa and I can search on it?" Arthur urged.

"Shadow Deep," she replied.

It wasn't very long before Pippa came back with some info. "I can't find that anywhere," she said. "What coast did you say it was off of?"

Bixby double-checked before answering. "Newfoundland," she said. "On one of the hundreds of little islands."

A few more silent moments went by.

"I must concur with Pippa; there is no record of Shadow Deep," Arthur chimed in.

Tipton shrugged. "I can't see how it's anything but that place, right?"

"It can't be that easy," Bixby said, tilting her head to the side. "Can it?"

"Random location in the middle of nowhere that doesn't exist in the real world: how does that not scream Level Two?"

"There's also the fact that it will take us weeks to get to the other locations since this submarine can go twenty or thirty knots at the most," Arthur said. "As such, I agree with Tipton."

Though the logic seemed sound, Bixby still shook her head. "I still say this is too easy. Something doesn't add up."

"I get what you are saying, Bixby, about it being easy, but maybe the hard part of the puzzle was figuring out to push all four buttons at the same time," Pippa suggested. "Or maybe just getting the sub was the hard part?

Bixby shook her head in uncertainty, but she also knew that what they were saying made the most sense. The voices started to jumble her focus.

"Everyone take your fingers off on my cue," Bixby said. The team readied themselves.

"One, two, three, off?" Tipton asked.

Bixby nodded as she counted.

"One, two, three."

They all released their button.

"Bixby, what if—" Pippa started, but before she could continue, Bixby reached up and cut the Tako communication. One less voice was better. She then closed her eyes, sat down in the nearest chair, and covered her ears. She was alone in her head where she could think.

Four locations: one obvious, the other three improbable. One location gets her there in enough time for December 23rd, the other three were not possible. What was she missing? This wasn't a puzzle, as far as she was concerned. It was a multiple-choice quiz. Maybe, everyone else was right?

Bixby sat up ready to make a choice. She was feeling rushed, but she wasn't sure how falling behind would play into this riddle and felt as if she needed to make a move.

"I can't think of any logical reason for the answer to be any other place," she said. "So, let's do Shadow Deep."

Everyone nodded, and Bixby pushed the button over the mysterious island.

The globe zoomed in on their current location and where they were going. When it finished adjusting, green letters typed across the page.

PLEASE CHOOSE YOUR ROUTE

Bixby was confused at the command; there was a blinking arrow where they were on the map, and one where they were going.

"Didn't you push Shadow Deep?" Tipton asked as he made his way into a position where he could see what she was looking at better.

"I did," she replied. She was looking over the map for any hidden clues or secret coding to see if she missed something. She didn't see anything, but worry and doubt still took hold of her. "Did I make a mistake?"

Nobody said anything.

"Then then let's try this again," she said, reaching up and dragging the arrow where they were currently over to the blinking light indicating the location of Shadow Deep. The map created a dotted line between the two locations and the ship gave out another jolt as it jumped into motion. Bixby and Arthur were more prepared to brace themselves with the ship's walls, while they watched Tipton bounce off a control panel and onto the floor.

"I'm okay!" he said leaping to his feet and taking a seat in the closest chair.

"Arthur, any idea how long it will take to get there?" Bixby asked as she too pushed herself up.

"By my calculations based on how long it took us to get to Tipton's? I'd say we have eight hours," he replied.

"That puts us there at five a.m. on December 23rd," Bixby said after checking the clock.

Arthur smiled. "Which puts us on time, it seems."

"I think that just turned on," Tipton said, pointing behind Bixby as everyone finished regaining their footing.

A monitor in a small corner of the bridge had illuminated and was rhythmically beeping. It slowly lit up a shade of green overlaid upon black. Neon green letters started to spill out onto its screen.

Congratulations Team Pinnacle Manor,

I'm so happy that you are successfully on your way to Shadow Deep in time for the Shadow Ball. There we hope you have fun solving the Level Two riddle. Remember, this level will be harder than the last.

Level Two requires different rules than the first:

All riddles are hidden inside the level, and you may take many different paths to discover them.

This level has multiple Red Herrings in it.

You must wear the outfit provided for you in your closet to fit the attire for the evening. You may not change out of them at any time.

You will find that I will provide you only one way out.

You may start solving the Level the moment you arrive at the Castle of Shadow Deep regardless of whether or not the other players have arrived.

The last contestant to successfully solve Level Two will be eliminated from the Riddle.

I have opened up your sleeping quarters, but make sure to close up before you make your journey to the Castle of Shadow Deep.

Godspeed to you,
Cody Dragonthorp

"Well, Miss Timmons, I think we can be certain that we are indeed now on the right course," Arthur said.

CHAPTER 10
FALSE START

"We have to wait?" Tipton exclaimed. "Gah! I'm already going stir crazy in here."

"I'm not sure there is much else we can do until we arrive," Bixby said as she headed down the hallway to the rooms that were previously locked.

Tipton looked up from his spot among empty bags of junk food he'd grabbed from the mess hall. "Where are you going?"

"To rest," she replied. "You should, too. We're going to need to hit the ground running the moment we get there."

Tipton straightened. "We have rooms?"

Bixby nodded, and with that, he grabbed the handle of his luggage and followed her down the narrow corridor. At the very end, the two doors were now marked with Bixby's and Tipton's names. They stood in front of their respective thresholds.

"On the count of three we open the door?" he asked.

"What is it with you and counting to three?" she replied, shooting him a confused look. "They're just our rooms."

"Yeah, well, you say that," he countered. "But what if there's a massive riddle or something we need to solve on the other side?"

Bixby rolled her eyes. "Really? So, what if there is?"

Tipton deflated a little before offering a sheepish grin and a shrug. "I think, maybe, my nerves are getting to me, what with Level Two and all. So, uh, one, two, three?"

With that, he flung the door open and ran through.

A split second later, his voice came bellowing through the air. "WHOA! This room is sweet! Mine has a fridge! Does yours have a fridge?"

Excited and intrigued, Bixby opened her door and entered her room. Sadly, what lay on the other side wasn't nearly as exciting as when she walked into her room at Pinnacle Manor for the first time. The room here was barely eight by eight, walls bare and grey.

"I can't believe he gets the cool room," she huffed.

She then went back outside, doublechecked that her name was indeed on the name plate (how dumb would she have felt if she'd somehow went into a utility room thinking that was her spot to crash) and called out to her friend. "Tipton?"

He didn't answer, but his door was slightly ajar.

Bixby went to his cabin and found it similar to hers, only this one had been well prepared for a guest. Just inside and off to the right was a door that led into a bathroom. To the left there seemed to be a closet door, a desk with a small sitting stool, and a mini fridge. Directly across from her, the wall had also been pushed up to expose a nook with a twin bed built into the bulkhead of the sub. Above the bed was a TV that you could watch while laying down, and in the center of the bed was Tipton, completely passed out.

"Adrenaline crash," she said with a grunt. Bixby knew how easy it was to sleep after getting a jolt of riddle-solving adrenaline. The gentle swaying of the sub probably didn't help either.

With that, she went back to her own quarters, inspected the now obvious seams, and knowing what she had to do, began opening each one. Everything she was going to use had been tucked away behind compartments and spaces within the walls. It didn't take her long to open them all up.

As she did, she chuckled that they included a closet and drawers for luggage that she didn't bring. She opened them anyway and inspected the inside. They held mostly plain clothes that she was sure would fit her, which was tempting to change into because she had been in her outfit for over a day now. She decided to finish exploring first. In doing so, she also revealed a hidden surprise tucked neatly inside the closet.

Hanging on the rod was a single black garment bag. Bixby couldn't help but to be curious about its contents, so she pulled it from the rack. Laying it out on the bed, she unzipped the contents.

"Wow," she gulped, pulling an outfit from within.

"This is the most beautiful dress I have ever seen," she whispered as she ran her fingers over the fabric. It was forest green with white and grey trim. The entire dress was stitched with silver designs, including down the long sleeves. A soft fur shawl was draped over the shoulders of the hanger. It wasn't like the futuristic dresses that were in style, which Bixby found too revealing and too tacky.

This gown had an older feel to it. It was almost as if it were made for the holiday season but also to keep her warm. There was something about the world's perception of style before technology exploded and clothing trends changed almost weekly. With Padrodian outfits, men and women could change how they looked simply by uploading a digital file. Bixby had always had a respect for something that was imagined, laid out, handcrafted, and original. It was a craft her grandfather practiced; Bixby loved watching him plan and build his puzzle boxes. This evening gown was something that was unmistakably one of a kind, and she loved it.

Attached to the hanger was a note.

Dear Lady Timmons,

We hope that you enjoy this handmade dress for your party. The gown's mask is in a black box above the closet. We look forward to honoring you and your accomplishments at tomorrow evening's ball.

Sincerely,

Staff – The Castle at Shadow Deep

I do enjoy the dress very much, Bixby thought as she reached up to retrieve the mask box from the cubby above her.

"It's also nice to know that Shadow Deep was the right answer to the Globe Riddle," she said more confident about their trajectory once she read the letter's signature.

Wish I could have gotten into my room beforehand. It would have made the solve even easier, she thought some more.

Grasping the corners of the box, she slowly raised the lid, and set it aside. The craftmanship of the contents made her pause once more in awe. What was inside was something that should have been on the face of a princess from one of her childhood books that her mother read to her. The base of the mask was the same deep green as her dress, and it was encrusted with what looked to be diamonds, that when stacked side-by-side, created the same ornate designs that were on her dress. The lips of the mask were thin and painted a deep shade of red. Feathers capped off the top of the headpiece as Bixby pulled the mask from inside the box, turned it over, and held it up to her face. It glided right over her ears and rested comfortably in place.

As Tipton predicted, her Tako earrings immediately shifted color to shades of green and silver that matched the trim and hue of the mask that adorned her face. Looking in the mirror, Bixby couldn't help but to think to herself that in normal circumstances she looked ridiculous, but in that moment, it felt good to be fancy.

A masquerade ball it is, Cody, Bixby thought to herself while looking at her reflection. What the riddle at the ball would be, she still had no clue, but she would look extravagant solving it.

As she went to place the mask back into the box, she noticed a Holo-Phone tucked in a nearby carveout. Pulling it from its home, she pushed the home screen and a green, silver, and white display lit up revealing only one app: a camera. She played with it for a few minutes and then realized that she had no idea how to hack this thing even if she wanted to. Bixby thought about showing it to Tipton, but just then his snore tore through the belly of the ship: it would have to wait.

Bixby quickly repacked the phone and her mask and finished preparing her room. As Bixby reached into Tipton's room to pull closed the hatch, something caught her eye. The corner closet door was open just enough to expose the garment bag that hung inside. It was similar to the one she had found in her own room.

Bixby tiptoed over and looked inside the bag.

"A suit?" Bixby whispered, now looking at a shimmery forest green blazer with matching pants. It was well tailored and matched her dress perfectly.

"Oh no," she whispered as her heart began to race. She quickly zipped up the bag and snuck back to her room in a hurry, locking herself in the bathroom. She could feel a panic attack coming on. Bixby's mind was racing faster than it ever had before. Tipton had a matching suit to the ball. He wasn't going to be helping her from the ship; he was going to be going into Level Two with her.

"How am I going to solve the riddle and keep him safe?" she sighed. Bixby closed her eyes and took deep, soothing, breaths in and out. They were supposed to be calming, but it wasn't working. The only thing that helped Bixby avoid stress was to do something to occupy her mind. So, she went to the bridge.

Arthur was bustling from one console to another as Bixby climbed up the steps to the captain's chair and started to clean up the candy wrappers, soda cans, and crumbs that covered the chair. She couldn't believe how much he had consumed in the little time he had been on the ship.

"Tipton should be doing that," Arthur said as he hovered over a large map.

"He made it to his room and passed out on his bed," Bixby explained, dumping a handful of garbage in the trash and went back for more.

Arthur shot a knowing grin. "Sugar overload, I take it."

"Probably," she replied knowing that it was more likely a mix of sugar and adrenaline. "Anyway, I think there's a power port on the captain's chair," Bixby said. "You should charge up, too."

"Thank you. I was getting tired of waiting for him to come and clean up his mess. I'm sure his house system loves picking up after him," Arthur said before going to plug in.

Bixby didn't have the heart to tell Arthur that Tipton most likely didn't have a house system or much of anything at all. The only reason why he had a Launch Room was because his father had died in an accident at Dragonthorp Inc. As part of his insurance policy, his son Tipton was to be able to attend the finest schools, which required a Launch Room and Holo-Suit. Bixby decided it wasn't productive to say anything, so she kept it to herself as she climbed up into another seat, cracked open a soda, and pulled up the old files of Level One on the screen in front of her. The idea of having Tipton with her in Level Two swirled in her mind, but the exhaustion from a full day of puzzle solving overtook her as she, too, fell asleep.

* * *

"Rise and shine party animals!" shouted Arthur while banging a large iron pipe against the metal interior of the ship.

Bixby shot out of the chair, disoriented, and dropped into a defensive stance.

"Careful now," Arthur said, chuckling. "Tipton! Front and center!"

Bixby plopped back down in the chair as Tipton made his way to the bridge, holding his head.

"Anyone have an aspirin and some Pepto?" he asked. "I really shouldn't have eaten all of that."

Arthur, though he didn't want to, reached into a medical cabinet, pulled out a bottle of pink discs from within, and proceeded to give him one. "I hope that will teach you a lesson; everything in moderation, my dear Tipton."

Tipton took the medication and nodded. "Yeah. No kidding."

"What time is it?" Bixby asked.

"Precisely 4 a.m.," Arthur replied.

"It's 4 a.m.! Why are we up so early?" Tipton groaned, dropping into a nearby chair. The sudden jolt up made his stomach gurgle loudly in a not-so-good way, and he grimaced.

"It is a bit early, Arthur. What is the plan?" Bixby said, still rubbing the sleep out of her eyes.

"In less than an hour's time, we should be docking at a port in Shadow Deep. I figure you will need some time to eat and get Bixby into her outfit," he replied.

"You mean our outfits," Bixby said in a monotone voice.

"Outfits? I get one, too?" Tipton asked. "But why would I need an outfit sitting here on the ship?"

Bixby smirked as she watched him figure out the answers to his own questions in his head.

Tipton's face went blank. "The only reason I would need an outfit..." his words trailed.

Bixby stood and fought to maintain a poker face by biting her inner lip.

Tipton continued to fumble. "You mean..."

"You're going into Shadow Deep with me, Tipton," Bixby finally interjected.

Tipton practically leaped through the ceiling. "I am! That's great! We're going to be the best team ever!"

Arthur cleared his throat and asked, "You have watched what happened to Bixby in the first Level correct?"

Without hesitation he replied, "Real encouraging, Bulldog."

"I'm going to pretend you didn't just call me that before I start making Bixby breakfast," Arthur replied turning towards the Mess Hall.

"I could eat, too, Arthur," Tipton replied with his real name this time in hopes he would make him breakfast as well.

"I'm not sure how it is that you are capable of eating after hearing your stomach bellow like a whale," Arthur replied.

"Two eggs, over easy, bacon, and the biggest stack of pancakes you can make," Tipton ordered as Arthur disappeared down the hall.

Tipton then shot Bixby tentative look. "You're not messing with me, are you?"

"No, I'm not," she replied with a small smile. He was so energized at the thought of being able to help inside the castle, she didn't have the heart to reiterate to him that Arthur was correct in pointing out how dangerous it could very well be.

"No more chitchat. Wash up. Breakfast will be served in fifteen minutes," Arthur shouted from the galley.

Bixby showered and put on some of the plain garments tucked in her dresser, then made her way to the mess hall in the front of the submarine. Arthur was in his usual black suit, but this time he was donning a white apron that said, "Kiss the Cook" in red letters.

"You don't mind if I pass on the kiss, do you Arthur?" Bixby said jokingly.

"It would have been funny if Tipton hadn't already made the same joke," Arthur retorted.

Tipton grinned boastfully.

"You don't get a choice here; eggs, bacon, pancakes per Tipton's request," Arthur said as he began to stack their plates.

"Any hot sauce?" Bixby asked.

Arthur made a face, a not-so-happy one as he served them their plates. "Unfortunately, yes."

Tipton made little work of making his food disappear while Bixby picked a little here and there.

"Honestly, I can't believe you can eat like that," she said, her stomach a little queasy from the nerves of what was to come.

"I'm a growing man," he replied stuffing another stack of hotcakes in his mouth.

"Your stomach was in knots like...not even a half hour ago," she said, reiterating what Arthur already said earlier.

"Thanks to Arthur's pink discs of magic, I'm ready to go," he said. "Plus, I eat when I'm excited."

That response made more sense to Bixby because she couldn't eat with the excitement even if she wanted to: they were opposites in that regard. Bixby still had no words at the spectacle of his eating skills. She could only shake her head in disbelief.

"Hurry now and finish eating. You both must get your dress attire on. If my calculations are correct, we should be arriving nearly any moment now," Arthur said as he started to clean up the dishes.

Bixby felt a thousand times better now that she was rested and fed—not only better but she had a small sense of excitement to tackle whatever Level Two threw at them. Maybe it was the thrill of the chase, or Tipton's eagerness that was rubbing off on her. Either way, Bixby's mind was gearing up for whatever lay ahead.

As she made her way past the bridge, she could hear the Holo-Writer playing scenes from Level One. It took her a second to find it under the navigation table: it had flown off her lap when Arthur startled her awake. As she reached down to retrieve it, the map caught her attention in a not so good way.

"Arthur! Arthur!" Bixby screamed as she looked at the map to Shadow Deep.

"What is it, Bixby?" he yelled back as he burst around the corner with his apron still on.

"How did you say we would get to Shadow Deep?" Bixby asked, eyes wide.

"I calculated that we would take the Strait of Belle Island and go around the outer edge of Newfoundland until we reached Shadow Deep," he said as he came around the side of the navigation table. "It was the most time-efficient route."

Tipton, worry splashed across his face, rushed to join them. "What happened?"

"I think we selected, 'As the Crow Flies' for a route, and the ship is bobbing through every port it can trying to keep us in line because subs can't travel on land," Arthur said. "So, we've ended up backtracking a lot, relatively speaking."

"No, we... I selected the path," Bixby said, slumping. "This is my fault. I got distracted."

"We can't be that far off," Tipton said, leaning in for a better view.

Despite his optimism and while the submarine had indeed made it a good distance around the edge of Newfoundland's southeastern ports, they were still far from Shadow Deep. He grimaced as he, too, saw how bad the error was.

Bixby reached up to the map and, from the sub's position on it, she traced a direct route into the open sea and then back into Shadow Deep's harbor.

A new message suddenly appeared:

PLEASE DOUBLE TAP THE GLOBE TO CONFIRM YOUR CHANGED ROUTE

Bixby reached up without hesitation and double-tapped. The ship rolled only a little this time. Bixby looked Arthur deep in the eyes and asked a question she wish she never had to. "How far behind are we?"

"Three hours," he replied flatly.

Her jaw clenched. "Be ready to run when this thing docks," she finished.

Without saying a word, she left the bridge fuming. She was convinced she would not have made that error if she hadn't been distracted by too many people trying to help. She wasn't about to let that happen again.

CHAPTER 11

THE PORT OF SHADOW DEEP

Bixby stewed on top of her bunk, fully dressed. Her mask sat in the box next to her as the minutes passed, all the while, beating herself up for her navigational folly.

How could you be so stupid, Bixby? she thought.

Bixby reached under her pillow and pulled out the one thing that she didn't leave Pinnacle Manor without: her grandfather's leather journal. Bixby had tucked it in her waistband in hopes that during her brain breaks she would read something in it that would spark a thought on how to open the cube. No offense to Tipton, but Grandpa would have been her first choice to join her in this level if he was still around. He knew riddles and puzzles better than anyone she had ever known up until Cody's virtual masterpiece. She opened it to the inscription inside the front cover just under the flap of the dust jacket.

To My Favorite Granddaughter,

May you be a hero to the people,
May you be a friend to those in need,
May you vanquish your enemies quickly,
May your imagination never flee...

~Grandpa Timmons

Those words always brought either a smile or a tear to her cheeks. This time was no exception as she thumbed through the pages of beautiful handwritten calligraphy.

The submarine's klaxon blared, and a red light began to flash throughout. Bixby stuffed the journal under her pillow, scooped up her mask, and raced out of her room.

"Tipton! Let's go!" Bixby shouted as she raced her way towards the hatch.

Arthur emerged from the bridge into the corridor as she approached.

"The computer read out says that the hatch won't open if you and Tipton don't close up the cubbies in your sleeping quarters," Arthur yelled over the sirens. "And Tipton, you need to change into your outfit!"

"You're not ready yet!" she shouted in shock turning around to see that Tipton wasn't in his suit.

With his faced turning bright red at her outburst, Tipton raced back to his room knowing he didn't want to delay them anymore.

"Why are the alarms going off?" Bixby shouted back.

"Evidently we are in the bay, and I must dock the boat manually," he replied.

"Want me to do it?" Bixby asked boldly.

"I've got this one. Please, go close up your room," Arthur insisted. He was not totally caught off guard by her bold request to dock a massive ship.

Bixby nodded and hurried back to her room. She made quick work of sealing the doors and latches shut. As she finished, the ship let out a frightful shake, knocking Bixby to the ground. The lights flickered off, sparked brightly, and then dimmed back to normal.

Pushing herself gingerly off the wall that she had shimmied up against, Bixby grasped the door handle and opened it to find Tipton in the hall, clutching a large metal pipe for dear life.

"Rough landing," he said with a chuckle. He stood there in a grey double-breasted suit that fit him perfectly. His bowtie was the same color green as Bixby's dress, and his shoes were polished so well that they looked like they were made of black glass. Under his arm he, too, held a black box with what Bixby assumed held his mask.

"Wow, you look gorgeous," Tipton said softly.

Bixby blushed at his compliment.

"Thank you, Tipton. You look very handsome yourself," she said as she straightened his bowtie.

He clicked his heels together and bowed in appreciation.

"But now we've got to go," she said urgently. "No time to lose."

Tipton gestured towards the bridge. "After you."

When they got there, Arthur was working some of the controls and gave an apologetic look. "Sorry. I've never had to dock a sub before."

"Should have let me do it," she replied before hurrying to her next question, "How long until we can go up?"

"I believe, now," Arthur replied as he pushed one more button. The system went dark. "But first your masks; nobody is to know who you are, per the rules."

Tipton's mask went over his head and clasped shut with two hooks on the side near his neck.

"It's surprisingly comfortable," he said. It had the face of a young man with a curly mustache and a smile. Just like Bixby's, his mask was green in complexion with very detailed jewel work. Bixby stared in amazement.

"Say something else, Tipton," Bixby said.

"Like what?"

"That's insane," Bixby replied as she slid her mask to her face.

Tipton cocked his head. "Is there something on my mask?"

"Just watch," she said as she pulled her hair back.

Instead of hair on their masks, they each had feathers of white that hid their scalp. That made Bixby very happy because her red curly hair would make it very easy for people to figure out who she was.

"The mask doesn't muffle your voice at all which is pretty cool," Bixby said as she fit her mask to her face and straightened the feathers down over her shoulders. It didn't take but a second for Tipton to understand why Bixby was so amazed. As Bixby talked, the lips on the masks moved with that of the person wearing them. The mask mimicked every facial expression.

"Whoa. That's cool," he said. "Wonder how hot it'll be in them, though. I don't like being hot."

"No idea, but I hope it doesn't get hot either; my hair gets a little crazy when I get sweaty," Bixby replied.

Tipton tilted his head to the other side like a confused dog but said nothing.

"What?" Bixby asked.

"You are saying your hair gets crazier than it already is?" he asked with a light chuckle.

Bixby slapped him on his arm and laughed at his joke. Then, the hatch above them let out a hiss and the handle spun. It groaned open, revealing the outside world.

"Let's go win Level Two," he said as he jumped on the ladder. Normally, she would have fought him to go up first, but seeing as she was in a dress, she let it slide this time.

"Whoa, you're not going to believe this Bixby," Tipton said, pausing at the top.

He reached down and took a hold of Bixby's hand as they both stood up on the conning tower of the ship.

Looking out over the port, there were beautiful snowcapped mountains as far as the eye could see. It was a lovely port with cobblestone houses and shops running all along the stone-paved streets. Normally, Bixby would assume that this town was bustling with people running from here and there, but today the town appeared still. The villagers had all gathered along the stone wall that separated the docks from the first row of shops. Each person held flags and banners that had the head of a lion in the center with words Bixby was unfamiliar with arching around them. Cheers rose through them all, and a band began to play fanfare music like the ones she watched in parades as a kid.

"Whoa is right," Bixby said as she reached the rail.

"You two might want to get the lead out," Arthur said pointing to the other boat docks in the harbor.

The towers of three more submarines peaked out of the water. The rules flashed in Bixby mind, specifically the one that said that the last one to arrive would be at a time disadvantage.

She snapped into focus and was already bounding down the rungs of the ladder.

"Welcome to Shadow Port, honored guests!" shouted a good-humored man. "I am Mayor Custard, and on behalf of the good folk of Shadow Port, I would like to welcome you to our humble home. You will be happy to know that all of the goods provided for your party tonight were created by the people of our town. It was an honor to be of service," he exclaimed with a bow.

Not wanting to be rude, Bixby replied on behalf of herself, Arthur, and Tipton, "I must say, that we are flabbergasted at this welcome, that we don't know what to say other than 'thank you,'" Her hope was that a simple "thank you" would hurry things along. Unfortunately, he kept talking and Bixby had to listen to see what he had to say in case it was important.

"For you to go to the Castle at Shadow Deep, we insist on you giving a speech that will make the crowd cheer," he said politely. "Everyone here spent significant time making the wardrobes, cooking the food, prepping the castle, and so much more," he went on.

Bixby whispered in return, "I would love to, but do you mind me asking how late we are compared to the other... guests?"

"Let me see, two of the boats arrived yesterday, but the guests were not allowed to head to the castle until the doors opened about three hours ago. And the third boat has only been here a short time," he recalled.

Bixby's anger went white hot. They'd fallen from tied in first to three hours behind and in last.

"Then please, lead us to where we have to give a speech," she urged with a forced smile.

"A speech that must make the crowd cheer," the Mayor reiterated.

Tipton tapped her lightly on the shoulder. "Did you just get tasked?"

"Did I get what-ed?" she replied.

"Tasked: like in a video game where you have to complete a challenge before you are allowed to move on," he replied. "I hate when NPC's bumble on and on about a task before they will let you do them."

"NP...what? Forget it. Is that really a thing?" Bixby whispered as they made their way to the stage.

"You'll know in a second if I'm right, and FYI, NPC stands for Non-Player Characters," Tipton said as he made his way to his spot next to the microphone.

Bixby's face soured. "Man, I hate public speaking almost as much as I hate heights."

"Our final honored guests would like to say a few words before they head off to the castle at Shadow Deep to enjoy the festivities," Mayor Custard announced over a small PA system.

"Thank you—" Bixby started as the microphone let off a high-pitched feedback squeal. It took a moment for it to go away and her to adjust her position to keep it form happening again, which just meant more time was ticking by, and they were doing nothing but falling further behind.

She tried not to think about it and went back to her speech.

"What a beautiful town you all have here. Thank you for hosting such a great event for us." She paused unable to come up with something more, so she concluded with a, "Thanks?" before she began to walk away from the microphone.

The crowd stared up at her like statues. It was as if the whole town was locked into place. Bixby tried to look and see if there was a way to squeeze by them, but there were hundreds of rows of people standing shoulder-to-shoulder blocking their way.

Tipton looked at her and tried to inconspicuously mimic everyone cheering.

Maybe he's right, Bixby moaned in her head.

With a deep puff of air in, and a bigger exhale, Bixby knew that nobody was going to move unless she made them cheer: she had been tasked. She only knew one woman in this world that was sweet both inside and out. Channeling her best Miss Marmalade, Bixby did her best impersonation.

"It is amazing to see how much pride you have in your village, and we are in awe of the beautiful gifts you have given us. We are extremely grateful for you and all the work you have put into serving us, your beautiful town, and the preparation of the banquet tonight at the castle. I am not sure we deserve to be called honored. In fact, I..." she paused trying to think about how Miss Marmalade always complimented people and Bixby knew it made her feel good at least.

"I think so many of you deserve this honor for what you have done. It isn't every day that people meet a stranger and give the best they can without expectations in return. As we go to Shadow Deep tonight, I will carry your generosity with me. As an honored guest, your hard work will be reflected in the venue, what I'm wearing, and even the festivities. You are all part of this night, and I am humbled that I get to represent the work you did. I consider each of you family!"

With that, the crowd let out a giant roar of approval and began to part. The human tunnel revealed a cobblestone path that could be traced all the way up to the stable.

Bixby's eyes flashed to Tipton who looked awestruck.

"Dude, that worked," he said with a disbelieving laugh. "It actually worked."

Bixby then noticed Arthur was somehow already at the stables, and he waved them over.

"Thank you again," she said once more into the mic. "But alas, we must go."

With that, she yanked Tipton to the stairs that led off the stage.

The cheers continued as they hustled along. She pushed the pace as fast as Tipton would allow her. After they shot into the stables, a couple of young men closed the doors behind them, leaving the crowd outside, peering in the windows. A stable hand raced over to meet the trio of travelers and pointed them towards a carriage that was waiting prepped and ready.

"Sir, the reigns are secured, and the horses are fed and watered. As you exit the stable, there is a path directly out of town that way," he said, pointing west. "It will take you straight to the castle of Shadow Deep. Also, here are your instructions to be opened as soon as you reach the bridge and not a moment sooner. Also, also, please do not force these horses into a full gallop; they are not meant for racing."

"What do we do with them once we get there?" Bixby asked.

The other stable hand answered as the doors to the road were pulled open. "You and your guest will attend the party, and the carriage will be looked after by the stable at Shadow Deep," he said.

"Thank you, boys," Arthur said in haste as he climbed up onto his perch. Once Bixby and Tipton were inside the carriage, he snapped the reigns. "To Shadow Deep! Heya!"

CHAPTER 12
HIGH CLASS LEVEL

Arthur's final instructions before heading out of town were, "You may remove your masks for a while once we have made our way out of the village."

Bixby could see miles and miles of open countryside, so she slipped off her disguise, put it on the seat next to her, and searched the inside of the carriage.

"What are you doing?" Tipton said as she crawled under his feet.

"Is anybody there?" Bixby asked.

"Yeah. Me," Tipton said.

"No, not you, silly, I turned on my earpiece," Bixby replied. "The last level started inside of a limo. I am just trying to be safe and make sure this isn't also part of the Riddle."

"Good thinking," Tipton said as he threw off his mask, and he, too, began to take inventory of their surroundings.

"Hello, Bixby?" a familiar voice rang over her earpiece.

"Pippa!" Bixby said, glad that the Takos were still working.

"Tell her I said 'hi,'" Tipton said at the same time that Pippa asked, "How's Tipton?"

"He says, hi," Bixby relayed before asking a follow up question. "Were you able to get ahold of my family again?"

"Okay, right, this is a business trip; no time for chit-chat," Pippa replied, sensing Bixby's urgency. "As for your family, I'm sorry to report that all I'm getting is jumbled code in response. I've tried contacting them on all sorts of different devices, and each time I get static, dead signals, or cutoff. I'm sure Cody is scrambling the communications so that nobody can cheat in Level Two with the outside world, but I'll do my best to figure out how we're being jammed."

"Please keep trying. Nothing about any of this seems right," Bixby replied, plopping down on the carriage seat.

"Do you think this a clue?" Tipton interrupted, pointing up at a cord that was dangling just outside the carriage's window. It was tucked neatly into the door frame and easily could have been missed.

"We'll call you back, Pippa," Bixby said, ending the transmission and drawing close to the oddity in questions. "Only one way to find out," Bixby said, reaching up to grab the cord. As she wrapped her hand around the line, Bixby hesitated. She'd never hesitated before, and it caught her off-guard.

"Everything okay?" Tipton asked.

Her response was a firm tug on the black braded rope. No time to debate the uncharacteristic lapse in exploration.

Arthur's voice came in from outside via some sort of intercom. "How may I assist you, Lady Timmons?"

"Say what?" Bixby asked.

"You rang the bell up here," he said. "Apparently, you pulled the cord that's attached to it."

"Oh."

"Going by your response, I'm assuming then you need nothing."

"Yeah. No. Sorry, Arthur, false alarm," Bixby replied, now frustrated that she'd apparently chased a red herring instead of simply seeing something for what it was: a piece of rope.

"For future reference, I would advise you not to touch that if you don't want me to stop, delaying our arrival," he said. "But if you must talk things through, maybe I can be of assistance Lady Timmons."

Bixby liked the fancy name Arthur came up for her while in her beautiful gown, but even Arthur seemed to be attempting to be helpful, which threw Bixby off even more. She was certain that on the sub he wanted no part of being in Level Two. Her mental debate quickly ended, and Bixby regained composure.

Tipton, however, looked ill at ease. "You look off. What's wrong?"

"Nothing," she replied, pressing her palms into her forehead. "I'm good."

Everything, however, was not good in Bixby's world. She had to pull it together and she most definitely could not let anyone else see that she was spiraling down, especially once they got to Shadow Deep with her competitors.

Focus. No more distractions, was all that she could think to herself over and over again.

"All we know is that it is a masquerade ball of some sort," she said to herself, trying to take mental inventory of what they knew.

"Are there more than one type of masquerade balls?" Tipton asked, trying to help her brainstorm.

"Yeah, but gimme a second to think," she replied. Bixby closed her eyes and tried to focus on only the things they knew at that moment for sure. She continued on as the wheels in her mind turned. "It could be a Murder-Mystery or a Who-Dun-It... It's all very different than Level One, and we haven't even made it to the Castle of Shadow Deep."

"Cody did say that this would be hard–" Pippa started to say before Bixby's earring crackled.

"I said give me a second!" Bixby snapped.

Tipton straightened, clearly surprised, as Pippa apologized.

"Sorry," she said. "I should probably go, anyway. Talk to you later."

Tipton had never seen her explode like that before.

Pippa was right. Level Two was harder, at least for Bixby, because she had never had to solve puzzles with other people's constant input, which, in turn, never gave her a moment to herself to be quiet with her own thoughts: it seemed to make things ten times more difficult.

Bixby reached up and grabbed the pull cord that connected her to Arthur but was impatient for his response. Before he could answer she was climbing out the coach's window to speak directly to Arthur.

"How much further?" she shouted over the clomping of the horses and a brisk wind.

"Hanging out the window like that is highly unsafe, Lady Timm—"

"How much further?" she insisted, leaning out even more just because.

"The stable boy said that it would be over that ridge," Arthur said pointing to the horizon far across the valley below them. "On the other side of that ridge, there is a bridge that will take us to the gates of the castle. When we get to that bridge is when you both are to put your masks back on, and never take them off. Remember, part of being at a masquerade ball is for people to not know who you are."

"Any idea what to expect when we get there?" Bixby asked.

"No, but I'm thinking the letter from the stable boy will tell us more," he said, patting his breast pocket. "I'll open it once we get to the bridge."

"You can't open it now?" Bixby asked.

"No," he said. "If I do, you run the risk of being disqualified."

"Fine," she huffed. "Just get us there ASAP."

After that, the ride was no more than a half an hour before Arthur rang over the carriage intercom. "Coming over the ridge!"

As Arthur predicted, the ridge hid a castle more spectacular than either Bixby or Tipton imagined. Bixby had seen castles before in the princess books her mother read to her as a little girl, but to see one in person was surreal. Up ahead was a long stone bridge that covered a cavernous valley. Looking out their carriage windows to the bottom of the cliffs, a river passed underneath.

"That must be a thousand feet to the bottom," Tipton gulped at the staggering drop.

"All that water is coming down from the mountains," Bixby replied in awe as she sat wide-eyed.

Backtracking the path of the river, they could tell that it was being fed by a waterfall that started on the snowcapped cliffs above the castle. A steady stream of water cascaded down from the peak above, and from there it disappeared behind the massive stone walls of Shadow Deep. The castle most likely used the fresh spring as it's source of water for the whole facility. Lost behind the stone structure, it must have flowed underneath the castle and out the front of the cliff upon which Shadow Deep was built.

"Have you seen anything like that?" Bixby asked, letting the frustrations of the Riddle melt away to a state of awestruck.

"Never," Tipton replied. "I wonder if Harvey can make Pinnacle Manor look like that."

"I hope so," she replied.

"Masks!" came a shout from the front of the carriage.

Both Bixby and Tipton reached under their seats and pulled out their headgear.

"My instructions say that when we pull up to the gate, you will be greeted by a man who will help you out of the carriage. You will follow him into the party. Bixby, you are to hold Tipton's arm as you enter. The gentleman will announce you from the top of the stairs. Then he will step aside allowing the guests to clap for you and pictures to be taken. From there you are to dance, eat, mingle, and enjoy yourself," Arthur finished.

"You just said they will announce us. If they announce us, won't they know who we are?" Tipton asked confused.

"I'm guessing they will announce you as one of the honored guest couples. Maybe it will be their job to figure out who you are," he replied, sounding confident of his logic.

"So, it's a Who-Is-Who party?" Bixby said more for herself than anyone else.

"I don't know. I'm simply reading the instructions," he replied.

The two looked out at Shadow Deep as the castle slowly grew in their carriage window.

"Are those gargoyles on the top of the spires?" Tipton asked admiring the darker aspects of the castle.

"Those are absolutely wicked-looking gargoyles," Bixby said, checking them out.

The castle walls were at least a hundred feet tall, ten feet thick, and the doors that opened as the carriage approached were fifty feet tall, cut into the stone.

"Wallaby World doesn't hold a candle to this place," Tipton said as they passed into the first layer of the castle. Now up close, Bixby and Tipton could see that what they thought was a non-vicious spring coming down the top of the mountain from far away, was indeed as grand as Niagara Falls.

"That is the most incredibly beautiful thing I have ever seen," Bixby said.

"I bet that river also turns turbines for their electric, too," Tipton said. His idea of beauty usually involved recognizing the engineering brilliance in a structure.

"How does this place even exist in secret?" Tipton wondered.

Bixby could only shrug, not knowing the answer.

They pressed through the gatehouse and were presented with a series of fresh-cut lawns, perfectly manicured flower beds, and neatly groomed hedges. Several water fountains spouted water in entertaining rhythms.

The carriage continued down a path that led to a tree-lined passage. Bixby and Tipton reclined in their seats, enjoying it all. A minute or so later, they entered a roundabout.

Arthur cried out to the horses, "Whoa! Easy now!"

The horses came to a smooth stop, and Bixby couldn't help but crack a grin. This arrival was so much better than his attempt at docking the sub.

Tipton looked to Bixby and wiped his hands against his pants. "Ready?"

Bixby sucked in a sharp breath and nodded. "Ready."

CHAPTER 13
WHERE TO BEGIN?

The door swung open, and two figures stood at attention on either side. A man stepped forward and offered Bixby a hand as she climbed from the coach. She replied with a thank you, but no response was returned. He was dressed in all white, and his mask matched his outfit. A small smile adorned his plastic face, but she could not see any features of his actual face as the eye holes were blacked out as well as the mouth and nose. Looking around she noticed the figures on either side of the carriage door wore the exact same attire. As Tipton climbed from the coach, the man in white turned around and began his formal march. Tipton held out his arm and Bixby looped hers through his.

"Please behave, you two," Arthur said.

Both Bixby and Tipton turned with a devious grin for an answer.

"That's what I was afraid of," he murmured as he flicked the reigns and the coach jumped forward.

As they followed their escort at a distance, Bixby was in full game mode and had her first small epiphany.

"Hey, from now on, don't use my name around the party guests," Bixby whispered into Tipton's ear.

"What are you talking about?" Tipton replied just as soft.

"If I say your name during the party and you say mine, the guests will know who we are without a challenge. And if it is a Who-Is-Who Party, we would lose pretty quickly," Bixby explained.

"Oh, right. What should I call you?"

Bixby shrugged. "I don't know; call me something fancy."

"Something fancy. Something fancy..." he said. Then his face lit with excitement. "Oh, I have it. I'll call you Buffy, and you can call me Wentworth."

"Yes, Wentworth. It's a very high-class name," Bixby said.

"Whatever you say, Buffy," Tipton replied in his best snooty voice.

Bixby couldn't help but realize that the building they were about to enter was two stories based on the two levels of giant windows. In each direction, the windows continued for at least two football fields.

"This place is massive," she whispered to Tipton. He nodded in agreement as they made their way up the stone stairs that ended at two doors that were both at least ten feet tall and carved with the most magnificent designs.

As they strolled through the front entrance, a red carpet was laid out for them.

"I've never had the red-carpet treatment before," Tipton said, feeling like a king.

"This is pretty cool," Bixby agreed. "Look at all the paintings of people," she said, pointing at the billboard of elite men in uniform and women in fancy Victorian dress. To Bixby they were full of potential clues but also very cool to look at.

"Do you think they'll paint a picture of us and put it up on the wall?" Tipton asked.

Bixby shrugged. "No idea, but if they do, I want it above the mantle in the Great Hall."

Two massive staircases, one to the right and one to the left, lead to an upstairs that was lit by torches. Bixby wanted to break from the man in white and do a little discovering.

"What do you think is up there?" she asked.

"Probably a room filled with metal armor, guest rooms, and a puzzle that will lead you into another adventure of peril and misfortune," he replied with a playful grin.

They continued on, and Bixby could feel the butterflies mounting in her stomach but said nothing. Their guide led them between the stairs, continuing to follow the red carpet. After about a hundred more paces, he reached a balcony rail. Bixby and Tipton stopped short, so the only thing they could see was the far wall which was hundreds of feet away.

"This place goes on forever," she whispered as she was trying to wrap her mind around how much time and work it must have taken to build a castle of this magnitude.

Bixby slipped her Holo-Phone out of the one concealed pocket of her dress and quickly slid it into Tipton's coat pocket with the camera facing outward.

"You got a phone?" he asked, miffed he didn't get one.

"I want to record this part, stay focused," Bixby whispered.

"Text it to me when this is all done? It will be a cool souvenir," he said

"Attention! Attention!" cried the man in white costume through the open space. The dull chatter of voices that could be heard as they approached was now silenced. "It is my great pleasure and privilege to announce that the final guests have arrived: let the festivities begin!"

The crowd let loose a roar as Bixby and Tipton stepped forward and stood at the railing's edge. The ballroom was filled with people looking up and applauding their arrival. Every one of them was decked out in costumes similar to their own with matching facades over their faces to hide their identities as well.

"Right this way," said their guide as he gestured them toward a wide stairwell that led down to the ballroom floor.

The stringed orchestra began to play, and people continued to dance and mingle.

"I guess the party doesn't start until we get here," Bixby said jokingly.

"Mhmm," Tipton replied. "If we get separated, we should make this the rendezvous spot."

Bixby nodded. "Clever thinking, Wentworth. For now, however, let's figure out what everyone here thinks this party is all about, and we also need to find Marin."

"Can we at least stop for a small bite to eat?" Tipton said passing the gargantuan buffet.

She saw his request as an opportunity to do a little investigating on her own, which was how she preferred to solve puzzles. With a nod of approval she said, "Absolutely," while patting him on the shoulder. "Load two plates up for us to eat and see if you can eavesdrop on any conversations that are worthwhile. I'll be back in a sec."

She turned to leave, but Tipton held her fast with a question. "Where are you going?"

"There is only one other place that I can think of with more gossip being spilled than the food table," she replied, pointing her feet in the direction of the lady's room.

"Ah. Yeah. Good point."

Bixby made her way up a marble set of stairs that ended at a fireplace. From there, the choices for doors were left to the oversized mask with diamonds, huge eye lashes, and full red lips, or to the right that flaunted a king-size mask with a mustache and a beard.

Bixby didn't need to go all the way in the bathroom because the first room she came to beyond the door was three times the size of her bedroom and covered in a hundred randomly scattered mirrors in all shapes and sizes. Each had a different design and frame style. Some were on walls, while others were around small stages so that you could see how your costume fit from all angles. Several were on movable carts while a few others were held up by similarly dressed masked mannequins.

She had heard of powder rooms before, but never had she been in one. Every few mirrors had someone in a stunning dress of every shape and size peering back at their reflections. Bixby quickly caught on to the fact that none of them were able to pick out their dress because each of them was either complimenting the choice made for them or complaining heavily about the choice made for them.

"I love the color of this dress," one girl gushed.

"Not me. I look like a glitter troll barfed all over me," another girl replied as she turned from side to side.

Bixby couldn't help but hide a smile in agreeance.

She found the most central mirror she could and admired her green dress once more. However, this time she was also listening to as many conversations as she could. Once she realized it had nothing to do with why they were there, she moved on to overhearing the next one, and then the next.

"All I have to do is post one photo of me in this dress to my monetized Holo-Connect, and I'll make more money than any of these stupid prizes they offered," a stuck-up voice said from a mirror to Bixby's right.

Bixby, curious about everything the girl had said, turned her body in the mirror to catch a quick look at who was talking. The girl was in costume, like everyone else, so Bixby couldn't identify her, but what she could identify was what was in the girl's purse, a small card. And not just any card at that.

Its title escaped Bixby's lips with a whisper.

"The History of Shadow Deep," she said, reading it off the reflection.

It took less than an instant for Bixby to realize she wanted that card. She needed that card, and so, despite never having stolen anything before, she began to concoct a way to borrow it.

During that time, the girl continued snapping pic after pic. Thus, Bixby decided to capitalize on the girl's obsession. She planned to walk over to the table where the girl's purse and card were. And then, once she blocked the girl's view, she'd pull the card from the girl's purse and set it under her phone. Then, once the two of them were done taking pictures together, she'd pick up her phone and the card under it and walk out.

It was a brilliant plan.

"Excuse me," Bixby said as she started forward. "I happen to be—"

Bixby felt her feet tangle below her dress, clipped by something. She barely had enough time to get her hands out in front of her before the ground came up and punched her in the chest. The room let out a roaring laugh at Bixby's crash to the floor. Immediately, Bixby tried to stand up and improvise, but someone spoke before she had a chance to redeem herself.

"I am so sorry for my friend's clumsiness. She was simply admiring how beautiful you looked in that dress and was hoping for a selfie with you," the familiar voice rang in Bixby's ear as she helped her up.

The girl took up all her things, purse and card, and snorted. "I'd rather die than get caught taking a picture with that klutz."

With that, the girl was gone.

Bixby's immediate response should have been to pull away from the hand holding her arm, but she also didn't want to cause more of a scene.

Before she could do anything else, the new arrival, the quote-unquote friend of hers, hissed in Bixby's ear. "You know, I don't think stealing from others is much of a good idea."

Bixby pressed her lips together, focusing her ire on the person before her. "Figures that Wesley brought you, Penelope."

Penny clutched Bixby's arm even harder. "I know it's not behind the field house where I was going to pummel your porky little friend, but I'm grateful that Cody put us together where you two can't unlaunch," she said.

Some of the other girls began to notice the tension in the conversation even if they couldn't hear it.

"Get your hand off me or I'll drop you right here," Bixby said.

"You've got me all wrong, Timmons; I'm not here to hurt you. I'm only going to follow you. A lot. Pretty much every second from here till...well, whenever," she said, chuckling and letting go of Bixby's arm. "Who knows what'll happen after that?"

"How did you find us in all of these masks?" Bixby inquired.

Penny's breathy laugh and shake of her head always preceded a rude comment, and this time wasn't an exception. "Because Tipton blends in so well, right?"

Bixby was eyeing up Penny for a quick comeback. She could see her full yellow dress and head gear that made her look like a giant yellow bird. Then it dawned on her: she hadn't seen anyone else in yellow. She had a hunch that she wanted to explore.

"You finished?" Bixby asked, knowing that Penny was going to try and follow.

Penny was actually taken aback when Bixby didn't try to use her words to fight back.

"Then I'll see you around," Bixby said as she turned to leave, but Bixby simply couldn't leave it at that. After only a few steps she stopped, took out her Holo-Phone from the secret pocket in the waist of the dress, turned, and snapped a quick picture of Penny with her scrunched up, confused face.

"Don't do that," Penny growled reaching for Bixby's phone.

"Oh, I plan on posting how hideous you look in that dress all over Holo-Connect when we get back," Bixby said loudly. All the girls giggled or gasped at Bixby's remarks.

"Delete it!" Penny growled.

"Not on your life," Bixby said as she darted out the door.

Chapter 14
Dance Battle

Penny followed Bixby at a distance as they left the bathroom area and made their way to the dance floor. Bixby stuffed a few blocks of cheese in her mouth as she reached the table where Tipton was not doing so well. He had noticeably started to sweat trying to interact with people he didn't know.

"I see you have made a ton of friends," Bixby said with a mouth full.

"I did talk to the guy in the rust-colored suit, but after he asked me a few questions, I froze. He asked me if I wanted to join the group he was forming to share information on tonight's 'festivities,'" he said using air quotes. "All I could do was stare blankly at him, stuff a huge glob of mashed potatoes in my mouth, and nod yes."

Bixby could tell he didn't appreciate being left alone. She, however, was beaming at all she accomplished by having a few minutes to herself.

"Well, I was able to learn that there is a riddle everyone here is trying to solve, and there is a prize for any of them who does it first."

"You learned that in the bathroom?" Tipton asked.

"Girls talk," Bixby replied.

"Boys stare at the wall," Tipton said in return. "But that makes more sense that the guy in the rust-colored suit was referring to a riddle... wait? Everyone is solving Level Two? Like everyone here, everyone?"

"I don't know," she said, eyeing where Penny had moved. "I was stopped when I tried to steal the clue."

"You got caught stealing?" Tipton asked, eyes widening.

Bixby grabbed Tipton's hand and pulled him out on the dance floor to get a little more distance from Penny. "No, not exactly like that."

Once they settled into a slow dance, Tipton went on. "Exactly like what, then?"

"Penny," she whispered. "She's the one in yellow."

Tipton tightened his hold on Bixby. "Penny Dagger? She's here?"

The two continued dancing around the ballroom floor, Bixby leading the way. She didn't say anything at first, but instead, took inventory of everyone around her. "So, I think I'm on to something else," she said trying to keep him apprised of their situation. "You and I are the only ones around in green costumes. I'm also guessing then that because Penny is the only one we see in yellow, her partner—Wesley no doubt—is the only boy dressed in yellow."

Tipton's eyes flashed around the room to see if he could spot dreaded Wesley. Penny was bad, but Wesley was worse.

"You think each team is color coded?" Tipton asked, putting it all together while scanning the crowd. "Do you have any idea what Marin and Greg's colors are?"

"No," she said, shaking her head. "I don't think they're here in the ballroom."

"Then where are they?"

The string music screeched to a halt as a bass drum started thumping from all around them. Everyone in the room was confused as it seemed like the musicians were confused as well.

"Look. There's smoke coming from those mirrors on the wall behind the musicians," Bixby noticed.

The center of the orchestra's risers began to split, and the conductor raised his baton instructing the strings to ready themselves. The beat was more intense as the mirrors opened and a wave of fog rushed out on the dance floor. A strobe light randomly flickered behind the man standing behind a table.

"Sweet! A DJ booth!" Tipton said as it glided forward in between the musicians. With a flick of the conductor's wand, everyone harmonized. Bixby's eyes rapidly flashed between the commotion on the stage and Penny. She looked ready to pounce.

The DJ appeared, wearing a bowtie, red suit, and sunglasses. Thick, black dreadlocks fell from a metallic mask, and his arms seemed to move with limitless energy. "You all ready to take this waltz up a notch?"

The band never stopped playing, but a hip-hop beat started to build with them. The crowd went wild.

"I've seen this guy on my Holo-Connect," Bixby said, her words nearly drowned by the music.

"He's amazing!" Tipton shouted back.

"Yeah, well, we'll have to play superfan later," she said, pulling him through the crowd. "Penny is guarding something. We need to know what that is."

"What are you talking about?" Tipton asked, voice now hushed since they were no longer next to the DJ.

"Listen up because I only have time to tell you once: Penny saw me in the bathroom trying to take the girl's card. She tripped me so I wouldn't be able to steal it," Bixby said.

"So, the riddle is on the card?" Tipton asked.

"Yes, this card," Bixby pulled a four-by-six note card from her secret pocket where she stored her phone.

"If you didn't steal it from the girl in the bathroom, where'd you get that one?"

"I noticed Penny didn't have a purse, but she did have a zipper to a secret pouch in her dress like mine," Bixby replied. "I was trying to steal her Holo-Phone, but like you, she didn't get one. What she did have was a stolen card from someone else."

Bixby beamed and held the confiscated treasure between the two of them, ensuring it remained out of sight from anyone else, Penny especially.

Tipton gave it a look. "What's the answer, then?"

"I don't think there is an answer on this card. The front has a history of the castle at Shadow Deep," she said. "And the back has three instructions."

At that point, she flipped the card over so her friend could see and read for himself:

1. Enjoy the Party

2. Solve the Phantom's Riddle

3. Take-Home Cash Prizes of $1,000, $1500 or $10,000

4. Drop your answer in the box at the front gate before you leave.

*ANSWER:*___________________

"They forgot a comma," Tipton said smugly.

Bixby flipped the card over to inspect what he was talking about. This was the first time Bixby was able to take a really good look at the writing without Penny scouting her. She held it close to her face in the low light of the room.

"Interesting," Bixby said before starting to look around the room.

Tipton cocked his head. "What's that?"

"One, two, three, four..." Bixby counted. "...fourteen, fifteen." She stopped and was now looking Penny square in the eyes. Her hand was inside her now empty secret pouch; her lips were pursed, and her brow furrowed in anger.

"Any day now," Tipton said soliciting information.

"Just a moment. I'm on a roll," she replied taking her phone out and pulling up the moment that they arrived at the railing at the top of the grand staircase overlooking the crowd.

"I don't see any other unique colors, but Penny was already standing by that panel," she said as she scrolled her phone and turned it so that Tipton could see. She then tapped her earrings. "Pippa? You there?"

"Ready and waiting," she replied, her voice filled with eagerness.

"DJ Doom is in the—" Bixby started

"I love DJ Doom!" she squealed.

"Focus!" Bixby insisted.

"Right. Right," Pippa said, regaining her composure.

"DJ Doom is here, and I need you to hack his playlist. Can you do that?" Bixby asked.

"If his system has pairing on it, I can try to pair your Takos with his computer," she replied with the familiar clacking of her keyboard underway. "Give me a second. Looks like it's set to private so that he can upload to the cloud but not have anyone send him stuff."

"All I need you to do is play 'I Dance Better Than You' next," Bixby requested.

"Hmmm, that is not set to be played for another hour," Pippa replied.

Bixby groaned. "I need it now, Pippa. Not in an hour."

"Alright. Alright," she said. "Working on it. How's Tipton?"

"He's about to become a whole lot cooler assuming you can get this to work," Bixby replied.

Tipton fidgeted with his hands. "What's all that supposed to mean?"

"The card I stole from Penny is our first clue in the riddle," Bixby said. "If you look at the one and the five in the prize money line, like you said, there is no comma. They are also both a little bigger and bolder than those other numbers as well. It's a common way to hide important words or numbers. To the naked eye that isn't looking, you could glance right over it."

"Oh, right."

"Thanks to Penny's stupidity, I now know where to go next," Bixby said.

"You mean she gave you a hint because she hasn't moved?" Tipton asked. "Even after she knew you stole her card?"

"Yep," Bixby replied with a nod. "She's right by the fifteenth sound panel from the grand stairway."

"That's got to be a door or something then, right?"

"Right. And that's why I need you to distract Penny long enough for me to slip through."

Tipton snorted with a half grin. "How am I supposed to do that?"

An instant later, the first beats to the most popular song to dance to on Holo-Connect hit the air. Bixby could see a small bit of confusion in DJ Doom's posture, but like any good DJ, he rolled right into it, not questioning why his playlist had jumped to that particular song.

"You're going to ask her to dance," Bixby said with a smile grabbing his arm and pulling him out to the dance floor.

"I Dance Better Than You" was a song where people entered the circle, busted a few moves, and then pointed to the next person to jump into the circle. Most times it ended with two or three really good dancers taking turns, but tonight Bixby needed Tipton to bust out the moves she saw him perform back in the library before the explosion.

"All you need to do is get in the circle for a few seconds, show your stuff, and then point to Penny. The crowd will get her into the circle or distract her long enough for me to work," Bixby explained. She then veered them behind a pole, removed a Tako earring, and slid it over Tipton's ear.

"What are you doing?" he asked right before Bixby punched the metal rod through his ear lobe: giving him his first ear piercing. To Bixby's surprise, Tipton didn't even yelp, but his face was in a state of shock.

"Now we can all communicate if we get separated: remember people can see and hear you talking, so make it as inconspicuous as possible," she replied as they kept moving and came back into view.

Tipton started to shake with every step they took. She parked him next to the kid in the rust-colored suit that he made friends with earlier.

"He loves to dance! Have fun boys!" Bixby said as she left him there awkwardly.

"No way! Green guy! You going to dance?" Bixby could hear the kid shout. "Awesome!"

Bixby smiled to herself and worked her way around the outer rim of the dance circle. When she stopped, she ended up being a few paces away from Penny. Penny, in turn, slid back a touch so she could keep an eye on both Bixby and Tipton, which was precisely the reaction Bixby was hoping for.

One by one the dancers bounced in and out of the circle. Tipton was petrified they would choose him but also knew what was required of him as part of the plan.

Tipton's hands were no longer clammy, but instead had rivers of sweat coursing over them. So much was riding on this dance, and so much could go wrong.

"Get out there," Bixby mouthed, brow dropped.

The chorus had already played through twice, and people had jumped in and out several times, but the song and their window were quickly fading. Bixby inconspicuously flipped on her Tako and spoke directly in his ear.

"Tipton, you've got to get out there or we're sunk," she whispered.

Tipton didn't move.

Luckily for Bixby, the guy in the rust-colored suit noticed Tipton trying to summon his inner dance moves. He slapped Tipton on the shoulder and started yelling for the person in the middle to, "Pick the guy in green!"

It only took a moment for the crowd to make the chant go viral, and then it was an all-out cheer fest for Tipton to be selected to go in next.

Even with all of that, Tipton remained statuesque, and all Bixby could do was stand there and feel her heart sink.

"You got this, babe," Pippa said, her voice sweet and encouraging.

Why didn't I think of that? Bixby thought to herself realizing he would do anything for Pippa.

Tipton straightened and life returned to his face just in time so that when the current dancer pointed to Tipton, he had it together enough to slide on out to the dance floor.

"Okay. Okay. I got this," he said, taking a deep breath.

Two beats later, Tipton was at it, losing himself in the music and letting his body move in perfect sync.

"Whhaaaaaww!" came the cheer from the crowd as Tipton broke into "Gotcha." It was one of the most difficult dances that was ever created for Holo-Connect challenges. It also required the person who started the dance, to summon someone from the crowd to imitate him in the middle of the crowd. He was going to try and dance battle Penny. Oddly, Bixby could see that he was enjoying the moment, not realizing Penny, the girl who threatened to take him behind the shed and beat him up, might actually join him.

The final chorus began to repeat itself as Tipton finished his loop of the dance and made the final gesture into the crowd right over Bixby's shoulder towards Penny. The crowd took notice and began to nudge her towards the front.

"No!" she said firmly as they started to cheer her on. "The song is over!"

She shouted, "No!" one more time, but this one wasn't towards the crowd, it was towards Bixby's escape. Tipton and Bixby were the only ones who knew the inside meaning of her cry: unaware of the real implication, the crowd was now urging harder that she dance.

Bixby slid her fingers along the panel and quickly found a hidden latch. At that point, the song had reached its big finale. As it hit the last note, the crowd struck a pose in unison. Simultaneously, Bixby pulled the door open, shimmied through the crack, and closed it as boos erupted from the crowd towards the girl who refused to dance.

Penny, no doubt, fumed, and Bixby would have loved to have seen her face. But at that moment, knowing all the distress Penny had put her and Tipton through at school, it felt good not to be on the receiving end.

"I'm going to get some punch now before I pass out," Tipton relayed.

"You were great," Bixby said. "You totally deserve all the punch you want and then some."

"Thanks."

Bixby turned her attention to the secret door she'd slipped through. She wished she could lock it so Penny couldn't follow, but there was no obvious way to do that. Instead, she ended up tearing off the outer edge of the note card she had stolen and jammed that piece into the door latch. Hopefully, it would keep it stuck, or at the very least, slow Penny down.

"Now let's see where you lead to," Bixby murmured, staring down a dimly lit, narrow, tunnel.

Chapter 15
The Boy In The Orange Suit

The space was so narrow that only one person could walk through it at a time. The faint light reminded her of the ones on the ground inside a movie theater. Bixby rushed forward with no time to waste. The corridor expired at a spiral staircase that led up.

"Up it is," she said to herself, springing up the stairs and through a narrow archway. She must have stepped on a pressure pad because the stone in front of her revealed an opening. She bounded through the narrow gap and skimmed to a stop. She could hear the rock rumble closed behind her, trapping her inside the room. In the middle of the cave was a boy in an orange suit. Wesley had to be in a yellow suit, so this was Marin's date or Greg. It creeped her out to see him standing next to an empty chair with a smile on his mask from ear to ear.

"Marin said you were clever, and you would figure the panel out on your own," he hissed. It wasn't Greg's surfer dude voice.

"Where's Marin?" Bixby asked, mentally assigning team orange to Marin.

"I must admit, though, I am disappointed in you; it took much longer than she predicted. I was sure that you had seen us disappear into the wall when you were walking down the stairs," he said before he gestured toward the chair. "Care to take a seat?"

Bixby side-eyed him as she carefully started to search the room while asking again more harshly, "Where... is... Marin?"

"Oh, Bixby. Don't you get that we're not on your team?"

"Where is Marin?" she repeated, biding her time as she continued to scan the room.

He patted the chair. "She's with her teammates. Now about that seat."

"You know as well as I do, she would never join Wesley and Greg," Bixby replied.

"On the contrary, Bixby, money does a lot of strange things to people," he said. He then covered his mouth with faux-surprise. "Oops! I've said too much."

Is that why she wouldn't return my messages? Bixby thought, recalling Marin's radio silence after they received their cubes.

"See, nobody gets paid if you get to the next round," he continued. "Therefore, I am simply going to continue to play my part and insist on you having a seat."

Bixby made a glance upward. Dimmed by the light that seemed to be missing on the far wall behind the boy, there was a riddle etched into the stone. It was tough to see, but she could read it:

What is Red at the beginning, Yellow during, and Black at the end?

"Oh, you see it? Here I thought for sure smashing the bulb would conceal it better," he grumbled. "It didn't take Marin very long to solve it either. She said you were an amazing teacher; well, the programs you provided her were amazing at least."

"You talk too much," Bixby cut in.

"The chair!" he said, raising his voice and stepping towards Bixby.

Bixby's gaze shifted, and she noticed two eye holes in the far wall. "Actually, I think I'll be on my way," she said.

"Actually, Bixby, you're not."

Retreating a half step, Bixby knew she had to make it past the boy to reach the eyeholes, which most likely was the exit.

"You could try to yell for help, but the giant waterfall outside makes this room practically soundproof," the boy pointed out. Now that he said it, she could tell that he was right, and that meant that the other side of the wall had to be someplace on the balcony.

The boy started to untie a rope from his hand as he made a lasso at one end, motioning Bixby to the chair again politely.

"I said, I think I will be going now," Bixby repeated a little more sternly as she started for the wall

The boy in orange sidestepped in front of her, "Nope."

"I am going to give you one chance to move, Orange Suit Boy," Bixby said.

The kid chuckled. "Cute name, but for the rest of our time here in this cave, you can call me Barnaby," he hissed as he grabbed both of her shoulders, which was exactly what Bixby wanted.

Marin had traded help solving riddles with some self-defense pointers. Instantly, Bixby jabbed him in the gut just below the rib cage to knock the wind out of him. He was momentarily incapacitated as she threw her shoulder into him as hard as she could, driving him down into the chair. Pulling the loop of the lasso over his head and down over his shoulders, she ripped the end of the rope from his hands, and with her foot in the back of the chair and a strong tug he was tightly confined.

His hands were loose, so he tried to free himself as he stood up, still strapped to the chair. Bixby swept his legs out from under him. The boy again crashed to the ground with a cry of pain, still in the seat. She reached down and grabbed his wrist and bent it forward nearly to his forearm. By continuing to apply pressure, she had full control over him.

"Don't move!" she yelled, pulling the rope tight.

"Ouch! Quit it!" he shot back.

Bixby ignored him and quickly tied his other hand and both feet to the chair.

"Now, how to untie you from that chair so that you aren't stuck in this Level for the rest of your life but keep you from annoying me the rest of the night," she said, loud enough that anyone digitally listening to her could help her.

Barnaby started to complain one more time before Bixby took his tie and stuffed it in his mouth, "Be quiet: I'm thinking," she demanded.

Bixby pulled the card from her secret pocket and reread the history of the castle of Shadow Deep in its entirety:

History of Shadow Deep

Forty years ago today, the castle of Shadow Deep hosted the most extravagant party the world had ever seen. Guests from every corner of the globe were invited to enjoy a night of feasting, dancing, and exploring all that the brand-new castle at Shadow Deep had to offer. Though nobody knew who had invited them, they came just the same to be part of the excessively glamourous masquerade ball. During one of the waltzes that night the lights went out leaving only one candle to illuminate the room. It was held by a phantom who stood at the top of the stairs. Speaking a riddle that nobody to this day has solved, he vanished with his final word. As the lights came back on and befuddled by his riddle, guests continued their night of festivities. But it was a grave mistake to not solve his riddle because that night a fire would ravish the grounds of Shadow Deep. The fire consumed the castle and the secrets that lie within.

Everyone thinks the Phantom's Riddle is the starting point, Bixby concluded.

She then turned her attention back to Barnaby. "Here is how this is going to work; sometime tonight there is most likely going to be a huge fire which I am sure you are well aware of," she said.

The kid rolled his eyes at her, but what he didn't realize was that as he slouched over, she could see the contents of his inner coat pocket. Pulling his stolen card from its hiding spot, she tapped him on the head with it.

"Barney, Barney," she said, mocking his name. "Then why would you have a stolen history card with one word circled on it… the same word that answers the puzzle written on that wall in a secret room of Shadow Deep?"

She held the card up to his face with her finger next to the circled word "fire."

"I'm no expert but being tied to a chair in a soundproof secret room is not a good place to be during a fire, even though that is exactly what you were going to do to me," she whispered with a growl in his ear.

He shook his head wildly in disagreement as he desperately tried to tell her something. Curiosity made Bixby pull the orange tie from inside his mouth.

"Yo! I had no idea that was going to happen! I'm just doing what I was told," he whimpered.

Bixby reached into his other jacket pocket and pulled out the Holo-Phone.

"Hey, that's mine," Barnaby pleaded.

"No, it's not. Guests of contestants didn't get Holo-Phones, which means this is Marin's," she deduced.

"Give it back," he growled, knowing she was right.

"I'll give it back," she said turning from him to conceal her next moves.

Barnaby snorted. "You'll never guess the password."

Unknown to him, while pulling up his lock screen, she was also listening to instructions from someone on the other side of her Tako earrings. To avoid suspicion Bixby took out her History of Shadow Deep card and began reading it out loud a second time. She was giving the illusion of studying the words, but in reality, she was allowing Pippa time to pair the phone to her earrings.

"Just one more minute," Pippa said as the clacking of her keyboard could be heard furiously typing.

Bixby slowed as she reached the end of the last paragraph.

"Alright, Bixby, use the code 51519 as the unlock code on the Holo-Phone, and it will pair with your earrings. I can't get you access into his phone, but if he gets within fifty feet of you, you will hear a beep letting you know the phone is trying to connect. It is a pretty basic alarm system if he decides to get too close to you again."

"Clever," Bixby whispered.

"Also, if you accept the pairing, you will have access to what he is saying and hearing. It won't take him long to realize that he has been hacked, so use your one pairing wisely Bixby because as soon as they know you can hear them, this advantage is gone," Pippa finished.

"Perfect," she said while entering the code. The phone uploaded for only a second and then returned to its normal lock screen. She began punching randomly away at the numbers a second time before turning back towards Barnaby, "Well, I didn't get into your Holo-Phone, but I did get the password wrong enough times to lock it for the next two hours," she smirked, sliding it back into his pocket.

"Really?"

"Yep. My bad," she said, inspecting his ear for com devices and ruffling his hair.

"You're not going to win this time, Bixby."

"We'll see," she replied as she peered through the eyeholes in the cave wall. It was indeed some corner of the outside balcony connected to the ballroom. The door would let her out behind a ten-foot-tall line of shrubs planted in an enormous, raised garden bed. The coast was clear.

Bixby grabbed the end of the rope and pulled loose the slip knot holding his hand to the chair as she disappeared through the back of the rock wall and latched the passage closed behind her.

Knowing it wouldn't be long before he, too, burst out of the passageway, Bixby hid within the shrubs. It was dark outside, and her dress matched the color of the foliage so well, it was easy to blend in.

Her hunch was right because Barnaby burst through the rock wall and raced into the ballroom thinking he was chasing her.

"You two there?" Bixby asked.

"Loud and clear," Pippa said first.

Tipton's voice came right after. "I'm here, but I am in a bit of a pickle."

"What do you mean?" Bixby asked.

"Penny has been tailing me closely since you left, so I went into the bathroom to hide from her," Tipton replied. Bixby could see Barnaby's orange suit was already making its way towards Penny and her yellow dress.

"Well, we need to come up with a plan because there is a boy in an orange suit that is about to come in there once Penny tells him the situation," Bixby said. Whoever reached him first, Bixby knew that part didn't matter. Tipton was in trouble.

"What are we going to do?" Pippa asked, her voice trembling.

Bixby sighed and shook her head. "I don't know. I'll think of something."

For a few beats, she watched the two henchmen through the balcony window talking passionately to each other. After a few seconds of heated discussion, Penny reached up and pulled down the glasses that had been sitting in her hairpiece. Bixby thought they were there for style, but Penny tapped the side of them, and Bixby watch as her thumbs began to text without a phone.

"She has some sort of Holo-Glasses," Bixby said.

"Those are a prototype myth," Tipton said from his hiding spot in a stall.

"I'm telling you she pulled her glasses down, turned them on, and it is recognizing her thumbs as they type," Bixby said.

"I can't hack what I don't know the makeup of," Pippa said frantically. "Get me something. Anything."

"Penny's too clever to leave a backdoor," Tipton said. "I doubt you can get in even if you knew what it was."

"It doesn't matter," Bixby cut in. She then relayed everything that had just taken place over the past few seconds. "Penny just stuck Barnaby on guard duty for the panel door and the balcony. He doesn't look happy, but he's definitely there."

"Barnaby? Who's Barnaby?" Tipton asked.

"He was the one I met in the caves. I guess he is Marin's date," she said knowing that it was going to be a burden to keep them up to date on all the things she discovered, but it was better than them nagging her the entire time.

"Marin brought in a date that knows Penny?" Tipton inquired.

"Long story. I'll fill you in later on it. Now, as I was saying, it looks like Barnaby's job now is to guard the two places that Tipton can go to try and catch up with me."

"Wait, so they are making sure I don't leave the ballroom to join you?" Tipton asked.

"I think that's part of it," Bixby replied pulling out the card from her secret pocket again.

"Why would they guard the balcony if they don't know you are there?" Pippa asked.

"Good question," Bixby replied, scanning her surroundings. After bit, she smiled broadly to herself. "Bingo," she said. "He isn't guarding the balcony. He's guarding the path up the side of the spire that I need to climb."

"You have to...what?" Pippa stammered. "Climb the side of a spire? Isn't it like a thousand feet or something to the bottom?"

"Thanks for the reminder," Bixby griped. "Either way, there are guards at the stairs that won't let anyone out of the party. I thought they were being good chaperones at first, but now I see that it's part of the riddle."

"What riddle?" Tipton asked as confused as Pippa. Bixby didn't have time to lay it out for them.

"I'll explain later. Just give me a second to think some more," she said.

Bixby read the card out loud making sure she was certain she was on the right path, "'Forty years ago today, the castle of

Shadow Deep hosted the most extravagant party the world had ever seen...' I think this constitutes the best party I have ever seen: check."

Pippa and Tipton listened quietly as she went on.

"'Guests from every corner of the globe were invited to enjoy a night of feasting, dancing...' even if that means just the competitors, it would cover that statement: double check," she continued.

"'Though nobody knew who had invited them; they came just the same to be part of the excessively glamourous masquerade ball...' not a single one of them in there knows Cody Dragonthorp invited them to be part of Level Two. So, that leaves exploring the entire castle, a phantom interrupting a waltz to deliver a riddle, and a fire to end the night."

"That makes sense," Pippa agreed.

"I bet everyone in there has already tried to leave the ballroom, and when they got turned away, they took the instructions literally: enjoy the party, wait for the Phantom's riddle, and then solve the riddle. That is why everyone is dancing instead of trying to escape into the rest of the castle: they are waiting for the Phantom's Riddle. They totally missed the fact that Cody also provided a clue as to how to escape the ballroom, hidden inside the instructions," Bixby said.

"The history of Shadow Deep is the parameters of the puzzle, the bold number fifteen is the starting point, and it sounds like the fire is the ending point," Pippa said, following along. It was a bit surprising to Bixby that she had caught on to all of her random thoughts so quickly.

"I do believe my final answer will coincide with the back of this card," Bixby said. "I also think that you need to leave that bathroom, Tipton."

"Why? You said Barnaby..." he continued to emphasize the oddity of his name, "...wasn't coming in here, and Penny is out there, making me safe right where I'm at," Tipton nervously replied.

"That's where they want you to be Tipton: if you are in the bathroom, you won't be able to record the Phantom's riddle while I explore the castle," Bixby replied.

"That's why Penny didn't chase after you: she was left in the ballroom not only to slow us down, but also to collect the Phantom's riddle," Pippa added.

Bixby nodded. "Yep, and that is why I need you out there on the dance floor, Tipton. Without your help, the chance of winning Level Two is nearly impossible. You said you were all-in Tipton: now's your time to shine."

As she finished, she stuffed the card back in her pocket and slipped out from her hiding spot and towards the first foothold. Hopefully, her words of encouragement would do the trick.

"You're right. I can do this," Tipton quietly replied.

Bixby stopped a couple paces from where she'd been. "Pippa, can you keep trying to get ahold of Pinnacle Manor?"

"Yeah. On it."

Over her earpiece, Bixby then heard the latches to a bathroom door flip. Tipton, no doubt, was on the move. A thought that proved true a heartbeat later.

"Green Suit Guy!" someone cried out.

Tipton's voice, enthusiastic, followed right on its heels. "Rusty!"

Bixby chuckled at how boys were good at giving each other rather silly nicknames. She also felt better that Rusty might provide a little protection for Tipton while alone in the ballroom with some of her competitors.

"Alright, Tipton, stick with him, and you'll be great. I'll check in on you soon," Bixby said. With that, she turned off her Tako earring to avoid distractions, grabbed the first protruding brick on the side of the spire, and pulled herself over the abyss below.

CHAPTER 16
EXTRA HELP

If it were not for the extensive training Bixby had been doing during the last few months since Level One, Bixby was sure that she would've fallen off the side of the castle due to simple exhaustion. The spire narrowed as she went up. As long as she leaned against the building as she went from foothold to foothold, she was relatively safe. After what felt like forever and a day of climbing, she reached the window ledge and peered in. She worried that Wesley was going to be there waiting to push her off, but the room was empty. Getting her bearings quickly, Bixby pulled herself through the opening and scanned the room.

"This is never going to wash out," she huffed, looking down at her once beautiful dress. There were at least four smudges that came from pressing against the building.

The room had already been ransacked, presumably by the other four people who had come through, so Bixby didn't take too long to search. There was an open hatch door left with flickering light emitting up from it. Beyond it was a staircase which she quickly descended.

Bixby worried with every step, knowing that Wesley, Greg, and now Marin was leaving their dates behind to slow her down. It was, however, comforting to know that she seemed to be catching up even though the three other teams had arrived before her. At the bottom of the stairs, she pulled on the wooden door's handle to peek out, but it wouldn't budge. There was a window just above her head that could be pushed out like an air vent, but Bixby couldn't reach it to see through.

"The chair," she recalled, having seen one in the spire room above. She raced up and then back down the stairs with the chair from the desk.

"I have to give it to them, they are persistent," Bixby said, standing on her tiptoes to peek her head through the window. She could see that the other teams had taken a rope and tied it to the gigantic latch and over to the massive wooden hutch right next to the door. Bixby climbed down and pulled the handle with all of her might, but the door refused to move.

Bixby sighed heavily and began to pace, trying to come up with a solution. "I could really use an idea, Grandpa."

Almost immediately, a quiet voice answered from behind— one she didn't recognize. "You could pull the hinges."

The thought of getting caught had Bixby so on edge that she instinctively grabbed the chair, spun around, and pointed it at the shadowy figure.

"Whoa, whoa, whoa," he whisper-shouted at Bixby's attack stance. "First, I'm a hologram so that won't do anything to me, and second we are on the same team."

"Who are you?" she whisper-shouted back: every hair on her neck was standing at attention, as she held her position.

"I'm Hemsley. Pippa's cousin," he said. "She asked me to launch in to help you find riddles."

The person stepped forward, hands up, and Bixby immediately thrust the chair forward to keep him at bay. It went through him like the ghost of Tipton when he launched into Pinnacle Manor, but Hemsley instinctively took a step backwards. Once he had retreated, Bixby tried connecting to Pippa.

"Did you send someone in to help?" she asked before Pippa could give her usually cheery greeting.

"Wow, that was faster than I expected," she said, chuckling. "Yeah. I did. I was going to launch myself in with the coin in your Takos, but who would do all the amazing computer work. Am I right?" she asked, nonchalantly.

"Who is this guy?" Bixby insisted.

"Oh, yeah, he is my cousin, Hemsley. I promise he'll be of help. He's one of the best in our little Cody fan club, and I trust him with my life."

"Ugh," Bixby groaned. "I don't care if he's the best of the best of the best in your club. Ask me next time before you just send someone in like that."

"Right, sorry," she apologized. "I was just thinking that he'd be really handy to use against whoever tries to slow you down. Or at the very least, a look out."

She hated the idea of having someone else giving input, but a lookout might be helpful.

"Fine," Bixby said. "I'll figure something out."

With that, she killed the communication link, and without lowering the chair, she directed her attention to Hemsley. "Alright you. Come into the light so I can get a better look at you."

He took a final, slow step forward with his hand defensively still outstretched.

Bixby was expecting someone who fit her preconceived notion of a hacking nerd like Pippa: a tall skinny guy with super thick glasses, acne, dressed like they were ready to attend a comic book convention, or, heaven forbid, another Tipton. What she didn't expect was the best blend of all of her mental images. Standing at the base of the stone staircase was a boy her age reaching just shy of six feet tall with dark hair and black stylish rimmed glasses. He wore a t-shirt of a comic book action hero, The Flagrant Shadow, and he was definitely bigger in stature than most of the guys her age, but in a good way.

"Sorry I scared you," he said.

Bixby put the chair down next to her and swiped her hand through Hemsley's hologram to reverify he was what he said he was.

"I'm not scared," she then said. "I just wasn't expecting it is all."

Bixby took a moment to assess the situation. He would be helpful as a lookout if the other teams were trying to chase her down. Since he was a hologram, she didn't need to worry much about him getting hurt as he could unlaunch when danger came. That said, there was only one problem with people joining her team as of late.

"Fine, you can help," she said. "But above all else, I have to stay focused, which means the moment you start distracting me, I get to unlaunch you. So be quiet."

"Okay, but before this goes any further, I suggest you work on the hinges," he said. "They should pull right out without too much trouble, and then open the door from the hinge side versus the handle side."

Bixby nodded, following along effortlessly. "Easy enough."

And it was, more or less. The first part was done quickly, and for the second, she ultimately had to make a trip to the spire room to find a letter opener and pry the door open. Then, Bixby was able to squeeze through the gap she made without knocking the door completely to the ground.

The hallway was narrow and stretched far in each direction and disappeared into gloom.

"This place must have a million possible places to hide riddles," Hemsley said stepping out of the doorway and into the hall.

Bixby flashed him a look reminding him of her one rule.

"Right, mums the word," he said running his fingers over his mouth as if he were zipping his lips closed.

He was right, so she said what he was trying to say in a way that didn't irk her. "It goes the same distance that way as it does this way..." she said, pointing towards the Grand Staircase. "...and there is a second floor."

She spun in place a few times and sighed. "I wish I had at least a starting point."

"I think I can help with that," Tipton chimed in. "DJ Doom is playing a beat he calls 'The Wobbly Waltz,' and everyone has stopped dancing. The History of Shadow Deep said that the Phantom came out during a wal—"

Shrieks of terror cut him off.

"Tipton?" Bixby yelled. "Tipton! What's going on?"

"The lights went out," he said above the commotion.

A booming voice thundered over the it all. "Silence!" it yelled.

Though she wasn't there, she knew exactly what was going on, or at least, who'd shown up.

"That's the Phantom," Bixby gasped. "Pippa! Record it quick!"

"You bet," she replied.

Bixby ran back to the hutch and rummaged through the drawers searching for something to write with. There, she spotted some scratch paper and a small pen in the back of the drawer. She got it just in time to get down what the Phantom had to say:

"Time is known by the silent dark horse pulled roses love ash fox chase my glass of milk the vase of gods dance panel horseshoe upside-down behind the fallen snow under the gargantuan omnivore"

"This guy is really freaking me out," Tipton whispered.

"You think he could at least make a coherent sentence," Pippa added.

Bixby read and re-read what she'd written. After she came up with nothing from it, she returned to the conversation with Pippa. "Can you play it back one more time? I want to make sure I got it down right."

"Sure thing," Pippa replied. "Here you go."

Pippa replayed it, and indeed, Bixby had scribbled it on the paper exactly. It only took a few more minutes of work in her head for things to click together.

"That is brilliant Cody," Bixby said, stuffing the pencil and paper in her secret pouch. She then turned to Hemsley and motioned for him to follow. "Okay, let's go."

"Wait. You understood that?" Pippa asked.

"I sure hope someone did," Tipton replied. "Because I'm still stuck in the ballroom with a couple of goons."

Bixby clenched her teeth, knowing that she should push forward fast, but she also knew that a never-ending wave of questions would follow. For her sanity, she had to describe Level Two as fast as she could so everyone would be on the same page and quit bugging her.

"Alright, here's the super-fast version," Bixby said as she leaned around the corner of the first hallway zigzag. "I've only heard about elaborate real life puzzles like this called Boss Level Puzzles," she started, moving up to the next leg of the bend in the hallway. "It's like playing a video game where you get to a Boss Level. First, you have to obtain the key to get in—"

"The cube," Tipton interrupted.

"—Right. Then you need to find a way to travel to the entrance of the Castle—"

"—the submarine," Pippa added.

"—Then you need to talk to a crowd that won't let you through unless you give a really good speech; I got that one," Tipton blurted out.

Bixby growled but kept things moving. "Yes, after that you have to find the map and the compass to navigate the Castle."

"Which is...the invite card?" Hemsley said.

Bixby nodded. "After all that, you collect easier keys to open doors which ultimately leads to a final Boss."

"The Phantom's Riddle?" Tipton tried.

"Correct. It isn't a bunch of random words. It is a bunch of random locations that hide the easier riddles, which will help us unlock the final, harder riddle: The Boss," she said.

Bixby could tell they were studying the Phantom's riddle because Pippa blurted out, "'dance panel," meaning the panel in the ballroom.

"Exactly. That means I need to find all these locations before the fire starts because I believe that is the end of the night," she said, stopping at a door leading to a guest room.

As she pressed her ear against it to see if she could tell whether or not someone was inside, Tipton asked another question. "Don't you mean 'we?'"

Bixby paused frustrated with herself. Telling everyone about the puzzle meant they wanted to help, which also meant they'd inevitably slow her down or get themselves hurt. She didn't like thinking about either of those, so she made a plan.

"Yeah, we, but we're going to give the others a taste of their own medicine," she said. "If they think it's best to stay in the ballroom and foul things up for me, I want you in the ballroom too. With you there occupying Penny and Hemsley, the odds of us catching up out here are far better with Hemsley as a ghost that can't be caught.

"And what about me?" Pippa asked.

"I need you to track Hemsley's movement and see if you can make a map of the castle as we go through. Also, keep working on connecting to my family."

Pippa clicked off without further word.

"And we get to..." Hemsley started.

"You're the lookout while I go hunting," Bixby said with a grin as she turned the knob and darted into their first room.

CHAPTER 17
WORST NEWS EVER

Bixby raced around the room much faster now that she knew what she was looking for.

"Nothing in here," she said confidently. She then peeked out the door and dashed to the next, where she once again listened to make sure nobody was rustling around inside before entering.

"How do you know what you're looking for?" Hemsley asked, keeping his head peeked slightly out the doorway.

"I'm not a hundred percent sure, of course, but we're looking for portions of what the Phantom spewed out in his rant," she said. "In the end, I'm working on the I'll-know-it-when-I-see-it method."

A few moments later, the second room was cleared, and they moved on to the next. As they reached that room, Bixby filled him in on the rest of her thoughts: it was helpful to her to be able to think out loud while educating him.

"Time would refer to something like a clock," she said.

"Then there is horse, roses, ash, glass of milk, vase, gods, horseshoe, and so on," he said, catching her drift. "And once we find those, they'll help solve the main Riddle?"

"That's my theory," she said, clearing their third room.

"This should be pretty easy," he said confidently.

"These small riddles should be easy once we find them, but that could be a bit more challenging than normal with four other teams pretty intent on slowing me down," Bixby said as she snuck into the next room.

Bixby had stopped counting after the fifteenth room they had checked, certain that there had to be hundreds of rooms in the castle. At the end of their current bend in the hallway they approached a double door marked with a lightning bolt on the plaque instead of a room number. Bixby listened again for people inside. Confirming the silence, she slipped through the large wooden door.

The room was a jigsaw puzzle room. There were wooden jigsaw puzzles of all shapes and sizes on tables fit for kings. Each table was made of heavy, dark wood with lipped edges so that the puzzle pieces couldn't fall off. The room had bookcases labeled with titles such as mystery or myths. There was fancy leather furniture dabbled throughout allowing someone to enjoy a puzzle or relax and read a good book by the fireplace.

It took Bixby only a moment to see their second clue's location. Up on a mantle above a roaring fire were twelve vases with a figure hand-painted on each one. Below every vase was the nameplates of a Greek gods.

"Those aren't right," Hemsley said, leaving his post at the door.

"What do you mean?" Bixby asked.

"Aphrodite is the goddess of love, but her nameplate is under a vase with a picture of Poseidon, the god of the sea. He's the one with the trident," he said, pointing.

"The what?" Bixby asked.

"The pitchfork looking thing," Hemsley replied.

Bixby walked up to the fireplace and tugged on the nameplate which held firm to the mantle.

"I guess we switch the vases," she said, pushing a coffee table next to the fireplace so that she could reach the mantle.

"Which one is which?" she asked.

"Zeus has the lightning bolt," Hemsley said pointing at the vase and then the plaque. "And Hades is the god of the underworld."

One by one Hemsley directed Bixby to the correct vase and then the correct spot. He continued his instructions as quickly as she could place them. Bixby purposely saved Hera for last, but not after Hemsley made a mistake. After she'd placed Artemis, the goddess of the hunt, in Apollo's spot, she turned to grab the next vase, but a sudden burn on her arm stopped her in her tracks.

She bit her tongue to not scream as Hemsley ran over to see what was wrong. She didn't answer, but instead pushed through the pain to correct her mistake. It was only when the vase was in its right place did the pain start to subside.

At that point, Bixby quickly realized that this was much different from Level One where burns were minor and didn't last. Cody did say that each level was going to be more dangerous, but Bixby was already over being burned.

"Those are the same burns from Level One," Hemsley said recognizing her injury from the videos of Level One.

"Only worse this time," she winced, inspecting the damage.

"I'm so sorry, Bixby! I was trying to hurry, and I got confused. I had no idea that you were going to get hurt. That should have been me," he rambled.

Bixby shook her head and sighed. "It's okay. I'll be fine."

"Promise? It looks really bad."

"It does feel like rubbing salt into a rugburn," Bixby said. Her eyes darted around the room until she found the bathroom, at which point, she rushed in. There, she rummaged through the cabinet of the sink, and then the small janitor's cubby.

"Bingo," she replied, grabbing a tube of ointment in the first aid kit.

"I'm really sorry," he continued.

"No time for apologies; we've got to keep moving. Make sure nobody is coming," she said while she applied aid to her wound.

A quick pat of her arm and Bixby was back to the fireplace with the medicine tucked into her dress's pocket.

She placed the last few containers in their homes.

Upon placing the vase in its correct place, all twelve simultaneously made a full rotation on the mantle and then locked into place. The picture above the vases rose and revealed a riddle.

When I am on, you can see me,
when I am off, you cannot.

Magnify me, and I will catch fire,
in a foot race, I'm faster than sound.

"I would have said glasses, but I'm not sure I have ever seen a pair of glasses run," Hemsley said.

"Mmhmm. But it's not that difficult. Want a hint?" Bixby asked.

"Hemsley nodded. "Sure.""

"Okay, a quick lesson from my grandfather to me, and now to you: riddles try to get you to think of multiple things that fit one or two parts of the puzzle, but the right answer fits the whole riddle perfectly," she said. "So, if you think of something that only fits part but not all, you've got to forget about it and move on."

Bixby then pulled out her card and wrote down a word under the group of words "the vase of the gods," making sure to also scratch out that section of the Phantom's Riddle and then stowed the card back in her pocket.

"That's it?" he asked. "That's my hint?"

"For now," she said as she peeked out the door to see if anyone was there. "I bet you can get it."

"That was more a set of instructions, not really a hint."

"Maybe," she shrugged. "But I believe in you."

The two moved on, searching down one side of the hall, but had no luck in finding another riddle. During the whole time, Hemsley remained quiet, not sharing his thoughts. However, while searching inside a bedroom with a four-post bed and large wooden furniture, he popped his head up over the covers and smiled broadly.

"Light," he said.

"Correct," she replied, returning the smile. Though it was a small distraction to help him solve the riddle, her grandfather said, "Correct" every time Bixby solved a puzzle. That glimmer of her grandfather affirming her accomplishments came to mind and it felt good. It was the first time in Level Two that her anxiety had subsided for a moment.

His eyes went wide, followed by a smile that went wider.

"That felt pretty awesome," he said. "It is like cracking a really hard coding problem in school. What a rush."

"Then let's get back to finding the next one because, according to my math, there is a potential of nine more riddles to find," Bixby said as they finished their sweep of that room.

"The thrill of the chase," he said as he continued to spout off clichés. Bixby could only shake her head and roll her eyes at his child-like excitement.

Making sure the coast was clear, they peeked out the door. Like before, there was nobody in the hall as they raced across the thirty-foot space between one bedroom and the next. However, as they entered the room, Hemsley waved his hands franticly at Bixby and then held his hand up to his lips to silence her as he pointed to his ear. Bixby could also hear something faint once Hemsley brought it to her attention. Slowly, the pair made their way to the window from which the voices were coming. They crouched near the sill, peaking slightly over the edge to get a better look.

"Do you see anyone?" Hemsley whispered.

"I can hear Wesley talking to someone, but I don't see him. He must be in the room above us," she replied.

"I don't care that the Phantom is gone, and they want to help," Wesley said. "Tell them their only job now is to keep

Tipton from leaving that ballroom. As for you, if she's out here finding riddles against us... You were brought in here to make sure that Greg and I make it to the next level. Find Timmons and make sure she doesn't get any further."

The sounds of footsteps followed along with the turn of a doorknob.

"My pleasure," replied another voice—this one that froze Bixby in place.

"I'm heading to the waterfall. When I get done, I'll meet you at the stable," Wesley said.

The conversation ended, and then she heard something that gave her pause: the sound of something slapping against the window above. She wasn't sure what to make of it until a sheet-rope fell down from the room Wesley was in.

"Hide!" she barely whispered. "He's going to repel down!"

Hemsley unlaunched, and Bixby rolled across the floor and pinned herself behind a sitting chair. She could hear him slide down the sheet-rope, and then the window went from cracked to fully open.

Bixby glanced at her feet, and to her horror, she found that her dress hung mostly out of her hiding spot. As she pulled it in, there was a grunt and a thud of shoes on the floor. After two footsteps towards her, they stopped.

Busted was all that she could think of while waiting for the chair to topple out of the way and Wesley to be standing over her.

"Yeah, yeah, I know we don't have time to check more rooms," Wesley said to someone not there. "But the window was open. Figured it couldn't hurt to take a look...No, there's not much here. Yeah, I'm coming. Relax."

Bixby held her breath as his heavy footsteps clunked away from her hiding spot. She stayed there, not moving a muscle, until long after he'd gone.

It was much too close to getting caught than she would have liked, but now there was a much bigger problem in Level Two than Wesley Dagger. Bixby turned on her earpiece to alert her teammates.

"Maggie's here."

CHAPTER 18
KNOW THY ENEMY

Level Two had gone from manageable to terrifying in an instant. She sat curled up behind the chair as Hemsley launched back in.

"Bixby, we've got to go," he urged.

"I... he..." Bixby stammered, trying to force a sentence out.

"Hey, what's going on?" Pippa asked

What Bixby needed was to talk to her dad just for a moment: he always knew the right thing to say.

"Bixby," Tipton said, cutting into her thoughts. "I'm coming to get you. Hang on."

Bixby leaped to her feet, her heart stopping at the image of Tipton trying to scale the spire wall—or rather, the image of him falling from the spire wall.

"No! Don't!" she barked.

"Already on my way," he said. "Besides, staying here is pointless. Half the people in the ballroom could care less about the riddle or the money because their parents are loaded, so they are more concerned about dancing the night away with DJ Doom."

Bixby guessed that fact from the pompous girl in the light blue dress earlier in the night. She had to figure out a way to keep him safe without making him feel useless, because if he felt like that, then he was going to do something dumb: like climb a spire.

"What about the other half of the guests?" Hemsley curiously asked.

"They all want to win," he said. "You know, money and all. Some for college. Some for fun. There's a couple in ruby red wanting to pay off medical bills for their mom."

"That is so sad," Pippa grimly interjected.

"Well, if I help Bixby win a hundred million dollars, part of my cut goes to helping people in need like them," Tipton said proudly.

"Aw," Pippa replied at her man's nobility.

"Mhmm," he said. "Which is why I'm climbing this stupid spire so we can finish up this riddle hunt. Besides, Maggie won't be an issue. I've got skills she can't handle."

"That's it!" Bixby said, perking. "Tipton, you're a genius!"

"I know," he said. "But pretend I don't know why and tell me."

"Of course," she said. Over the next few minutes, Bixby talked with her team as she worked out a vague idea of a plan that was nothing more than gut feeling into something concrete. By the time they reached the end of the back and forth, the whole thing felt like a long shot, but it seemed at least possible, and certainly left them in a better spot than where they were before.

"So you guys do your thing, and that should give me enough time to clear the rest of the castle and maybe find Marin," Bixby said. "After that, it's the outside clues, and the final solution. Sound good?"

"Sounds good," everyone else replied.

As part of her plan, Bixby figured it best that she split up with Hemsley. Together, they continued to search the rooms in the hall, and it wasn't long before the two of them had gotten into a fast, methodical rhythm, and her confidence at winning Level Two grew more and more.

"Okay, these are the last twelve rooms on this wing, and then we try to find our way upstairs," Bixby whispered as they slipped down the hall. "When you're done, or if you find something, tell me through the earrings before you unlaunch and launch back in near me. I don't want you popping in at a bad time. You know, guards and all."

"Guards? Where are you headed?" Hemsley asked.

"There's a dining room at the base of the stairs. I am going to sneak in there before I go up to the second floor. Once I get past the two stair monitors, I'll let you know so you can join me."

"Roger that. See you soon," he said, before offering a salute. With that, he disappeared into another room.

Bixby darted, ducked, and slinked her way back to the middle of the castle building. She could see the red carpet that she had walked in on a few hours earlier. There were two guards: one stationed at the bottom of each side of the grand staircase going upward. If it were not for the dining room that she needed to go into, she would have climbed up Wesley's sheets that he left hanging from the second-story window; however, Bixby had a hunch that at least one of the clues would be well fortified. Like in any video game, there would always be one or two guards watching over the proverbial treasure chest.

Thus, Bixby's logic was to climb out one of the bedroom windows and back through the dining room window. That idea was nixed almost immediately when a guard entered the massive front doors and started talking to the others.

"Keep an eye out for anyone who doesn't belong here," he said. "Some of the guests snuck out of the ballroom. And don't forget to log anyone you catch if you want your bonus pay."

Each guard nodded before the first left.

"We are doing a sweep of the perimeter of the castle now," the senior guard said.

Bixby rubbed her chin as she stared at the door she needed to get through. It was in direct view of the two guards, and neither one looked ready to move in the next century.

"Going to need a distraction," Bixby whispered to herself. "Just like a video game."

Another few moments came and went before something occurred to her. "The door, maybe?"

Bixby backtracked to the spire door that was now missing its hinges. Bunching up the rope that Wesley and Greg used to tie the door shut, she squeezed back through the spire entry and reassembled the pins in their place. Now with the door fully functional, she tied a slip knot to it. Letting out the rope, she crawled into the lower cabinet of the nearby hutch.

"Man, I hope this works," she said, chuckling to herself.

She sincerely didn't know if it would and gave herself a 50/50 shot.

With a firm tug, Bixby pulled the rope as hard and as fast as she could. The spire door shut with a thud as the slip knot let loose of the handle. She continued to pull the rope into the hutch cabinet with her and closed the cubie's door.

Someone started coming from down the hall, not all the way, maybe a few paces at the most.

"Where are you going?" one voice said.

"Heard something over here," another replied. "Let's check it out."

"What about our post?"

"What about it?" came the reply. Then a huff. "Look, there are two guards at the main entrance, and two at the ballroom door. You can stay there if you want, but this is my chance to get in on a little of that cash he just talked about."

"Ugh. Fine."

The footsteps resumed, only this time, there were two sets of them. Then she heard the door creak open and the sounds of footsteps fading away as they went up the stairs.

Bixby quietly left the cabinet and snuck down the hall to the dining room door. She saw two more guards along the way, standing at the balcony rail with their backs turned toward her. Thankfully, they seemed to be watching the party below like hawks.

Silent as a shadow, Bixby slipped into the dinning hall. Her eyes darted as fast as they could around the room. Most of the space was filled by a grand table fit for a king, lined with gorgeous seats. At the far end was another hutch. Inside of that, she spied three horse figurines: one white, one spotted, and one black.

"Score," Bixby said, grinning from ear to ear as she raced across the hall.

When she got to the hutch, she practically ripped open the glass door that held the figures. Her hands snatched up the black horse right after, but once she had it, nothing in the room seemed to change.

Confused, she peered into the now empty space where the horse had stood. There, she saw several scratches on the wooden shelf.

I'm not the first person to find this, she thought.

She studied the spot further and noticed something had left the deep grooves in the wood. Finding that curious, Bixby turned the horse over. A golden plate sat screwed into the bottom and read:

I was born in the eyes of every man's desires. My enemy is contempt.

The world will, however, never let me die because I am number 3 of 7.

Before Bixby had a chance to think about the puzzle, Hemsley checked in.

"Bixby, I think I found something in a bedroom up here. It's a glass of milk sitting on a book, but I don't see a riddle," he said.

"There's nothing else around the book?" Bixby said softly in her earpiece.

"Just a book," he said. "But if the riddle is inside, I won't be able to check. I'm a hologram."

"What's the book's title?" she asked.

"A Father's Heir," he said. "Do you know it?"

"No, but I don't need to," she said. "The title is the riddle."

"It is?"

"Yeah. Think about it: what's a father's heir?"

"A child," said a distant and familiar voice from the other end of the dining room. Bixby held tightly to the horse thinking she may need it to defend herself as she let her eyes adjust to the figure who sat at the head of the table.

"Let's not kid ourselves, Bixby, these riddles are kids' games to you," she said in a complimentary voice. "It was probably ten times harder giving everyone else the slip."

Bixby sighed and shook her head. "Why did you sell out, Marin? You know they're going to turn on you the moment they knock me off."

"You don't actually know me at all do you?" she said with a snort

"I guess not."

"The only reason I'm in this game is because I was the only one in the house that fit the age requirement. I don't even want to be here," she said.

Bixby had no idea why Marin didn't sneak up on her and tie her up: maybe Marin was playing both sides. Bixby decided that either way, she needed to keep the conversation going and bide her time until she had a way out.

"But we helped each other in Level One?" Bixby said. "If you didn't care then, why would you team up with them? And what happened to boys against girls?"

Marin scowled, and Bixby continued, "I even said you could have all the money if you wanted it; I was in it for Cody. You knew that."

Marin shifted forward in her chair and folded her hands on the table. "I live in one of Cody Dragonthorp's amazing houses with a room and all of those perks. The only problem is that the house doesn't belong to my family. My dad is the butler because Plumberry Isle doesn't have H-bots. My mom scrubs the house and waits on the General and his spoiled kids day and night while the old lady of the house is living the life of luxury. I didn't volunteer for military school; it was the General's program, and he needed a guinea pig to test it out."

"I didn't know," Bixby said softly.

"I'm not done," Marin scolded. "I'm launched in my Launch Room fifteen hours a day with nothing but a future in a military that is nowhere near what I dreamt of doing... when I was offered a hundred thousand dollars to switch sides, I considered it. When they showed me all the technology they're using at Dragonthorp Inc. to make sure you and I don't make it out of the next two rounds, the decision became easy."

Bixby had no reply. She couldn't imagine having to deal with any of that.

"Don't you see, Bixby? We'll never win; not with Wesley, Greg, Penny, Maggie, and all of Dragonthorp Inc.'s resources against us. Not to mention the fact you've left your only loyal friend in the world stuck in the ballroom instead of out here helping you. You've made yourself one against a thousand from Dragonthorp Inc."

Her honest words cut deep, but despite the truth to those words, Bixby needed Marin to hear another side, too.

"Don't you see that they've no intentions of paying you a dime?" Bixby countered. "You were there on the ledge when Maggie tried to push me over. She said you were the original target because you were their biggest threat. They're playing you against me, and to get you to do that they're offering you freedom as a reward. You're in the military; what did they teach you about the honor of selling out your friends?"

Marin stared blankly, and Bixby grew more confident that Marin wasn't going to turn her in as she started to approach the other end of the table. They both had pushed everyone away for the illusion of safety.

"This Level is a sham for everyone that's in the ballroom. They have no idea they're a cover for Cody's riddle," Bixby continued as she finished closing the distance between them.

"It's even sadder because half the people in there couldn't care less about the money, while the other half are desperate to win to pay for college, or their mom's medical bills: they're the cogs in a machine. This con makes me wonder if the hundred million dollars at the end of this riddle is a sham as well. The only thing I do know is that you and I are their targets. Time for you to wake up and get your head out of the sand."

Marin pressed her lips into a tight line. "Maybe."

"No maybe about it," Bixby said as she made her way to the window. "Look, there's still a room for you at Pinnacle Manor as a sister, not a servant... and you don't need to check the bottom of the horse: the answers to both of the riddles in this room is 'greed.' So that makes us even again. Do what you want, but I'm going to win this thing no matter how much Dragonthorp Inc. throws at me."

Marin drummed her fingers on the table for a moment before pulling a pair of communication glasses from her secret pocket. When she spoke, her attention was elsewhere. "Look," she said. "This is getting silly. How long do I have to wait here for Timmons?"

Maggie's voice came grumbling over the comm. "You don't think she's coming?"

"If she was, she'd be here by now, assuming she hasn't been here already."

"Fine. We need to figure out a way to have Bixby come to us. So, change of plans: head out the window and clear the last quarter of the building. We only have four more riddles to find."

"Copy," Marin said tapping the glasses to turn them off. She then took to her feet and smirked at Bixby. "Looks like you still owe me."

Chapter 19
Distractions

Marin had leveled the playing field with the other team a little bit more. Bixby knew that two of their henchmen were in the ballroom. Two were outside at the stables or waterfall. Marin was a non-threat, which left only Maggie to deal with. They had four riddles left to find while Bixby guessed she had six left to locate. Even though she was behind, the other team was wasting resources by trying to slow Bixby down instead of focusing on finishing the game. She was within reach, and that made her feel really, really good. But with the newfound jolt of reality from Marin, Bixby felt a pang of guilt for not letting her friends help.

"Everyone, check in," Bixby said, connecting to them all.

"Ballroom is still divided between the party people and the study people, and my two personal shadows are still pretty upset that they are stuck in here with me," Tipton said, DJ Doom still playing with the band in the background.

"I'm sorry to say that there's still no word from your family. As for the glasses they're using, I think I may have broken into the research lab's database, and I'm searching now for specs on the specs," Pippa reported.

"I see what you did there," Tipton replied with an added pun to Pippa's.

"Okay, thank you, you two," Bixby replied with a sharp exhale. "Hemsley, FYI, I'm not going upstairs."

"You're not?" he asked.

Bixby shook her head. "No. There are two riddles outside I'm going after."

"Should I come, too?"

Bixby, well on the move at that point, ducked behind a row of bushes on the way to the stables. "Hang on a sec," she said. She then waited there a few more moments to make sure it was safe before giving him the signal. "Alright. We're good to go. Pop out and launch back in."

A couple of heartbeats passed, and then Hemsley was at her side. "Good deal. What's the plan on this one?"

"I don't really have one," she admitted. "I'm operating on hunches. Besides, there's too many rooms to methodically search them all at this point. So, we're headed for the stables"

"Horseshoe upside-down?" he asked.

"Can't imagine a better place there'd be one," she said as the pair eased forward.

When they finally got to the stables, they saw a farmhand inside who was caring for the horses.

"We've got to get him out of here," Bixby said as she tried to formulate a distraction. She didn't have to think long because out of a stall darted a massive white and black horse, rippling with muscles.

Immediately, the farmhand gave chase. "Whoa! Whoa! Get back here!"

"Well, that was easy," Hemsley whispered as he began to stand up.

Bixby reached up and quickly turned her earrings off which also unlaunched Hemsley.

She sat in the silence as the sound of the farm hand grew faint.

"Easy enough," Greg's surfer dude voice rang through the stable.

Bixby looked through a small hole in the wall, where a knot had long since rotted out. Standing next to Greg was Wesley.

"Alright, let's get to that horseshoe and give it a turn," Wesley said, rubbing his hands together.

Bixby watched the two take an end of a large barrel and shimmied it underneath the middle post in the stable. Wesley climbed on top of it and reached a horseshoe that was neatly tucked in the shadows. With both hands, he turned it from right-side-up to upside-down.

A loud clack echoed through the stables, stirring the horses. Because Greg was already on the ground, he reached the riddle first. One of the stable chests had popped open, and a riddle must have been written under the lid.

"Get Marin on the line to solve this," Greg said.

Wesley slipped on a pair of glasses and tapped the side.

"Tell her, 'Feed me I live. Give me drink, and I die.'" Greg instructed

Wesley shook his head and laughed. "No need. That's easy. It's fire."

Bixby mouthed the word "fire" as Wesley said it aloud.

"Hey! What are you two doing?" the farmhand yelled as he pulled the wayward horse back to its stall.

"I—I mean, we—" Wesley stammered.

But that was all he got out. The man turned his head over his shoulder and yelled. "Guards!"

Bixby, who'd further hidden herself in the shrubs, stayed deathly still.

"Listen kids, back to the party," the first guard growled. "I'm not in the mood for games."

"Well, we are," Greg shouted as he and Wesley bolted free and ran for the garden maze.

The guards immediate gave chase.

Once they were gone, Bixby pulled out her card. scribbled the answer to "horseshoe upside-down," and put a line through that portion of the phantom's riddle.

"Three to five," she said, keeping a score of how many riddles everyone had left to solve.

The sound of the chest being relatched made Bixby peek in the stable once more. The farmhand was already back to work caring for the horses.

"I'm sorry they scared you, girl," he said as patted the top of the animal's head. "But at least it was you, right? And not the two at the end? Never would've caught those speed demons."

A few more minutes passed as the man finished doing whatever he'd been up to, and then once again, Bixby found herself alone.

"You can relaunch, Hemsley, but be quiet," Bixby said, turning her Tako back on. "How are the rest of you holding up?"

"Bixby?" Tipton asked.

"Yeah? What's up?" she replied.

"I did exactly what you said, and Barnaby moved from guarding the spire so he could meet Penny inside," Tipton said, sounding surprised that her scheme was working. "What's next?"

"Make sure you keep an eye on them, and stay calm," she said right as Hemsley appeared next to her.

Tipton snorted. "That's what people say right before spiders and snakes jump out."

"They won't this time. Promise," Bixby said. "Just stick to the plan."

Pippa didn't come on the line, which was a bit strange to Bixby, but she couldn't worry about that now. Turning back to Hemsley and pulling out her copy of the Phantom's riddle, Bixby had a hunch where to find one of the five remaining riddles on her list.

Time is known by the silent dark horse pulled roses love ash fox chase my glass of milk the vase of gods dance panel horseshoe upside-down behind the fallen snow under the gargantuan omnivore

"We need to get behind the waterfalls," Bixby said.

"Behind the fallen snow?" Hemsley asked as he looked at his copy of the Phantom's riddle.

Bixby nodded. "Yep. That's what I'm thinking."

From up on the ridge where the stables stood, they could see that it wasn't far to a large hedge line that looked to lead back to the waterfalls. There were guards above the ridge as Bixby and Hemsley crept along the stone walls of the stable.

"We are going to have to do a brilliant job of sneaking behind that waterfall," Hemsley whispered.

"We also can't talk once we get in there," she said as she focused on how tight the guards were scanning.

Bixby saw a gate marked "EMPLOYEE'S ENTRANCE" which seemed to lead right to the pond that the waterfall made. The other option was a continuation of the hedge maze that Wesley and Greg had darted into earlier.

Hemsley shrugged at the choice, so Bixby signaled to him that they were going to go through the gardens. To her, it seemed like the more concealed path.

Starting down an ornate trail of wildflowers, trees, and high shrubbery, the pair headed in the general direction of the waterfall. The maze was vast and well designed. It had plenty of wrong turns and dead ends that had Bixby frustrated because she didn't have time to memorize the maze. According to the history of Shadow Deep, there was going to be a fire sometime tonight, and the other teams had more answers than she did. Bixby raced through the turns as fast as she could, but there were guards also watching from above which led to many pauses as they dashed between hedges.

"I have an idea, Bixby," Hemsley said.

"Hurry up with it because we don't have time for grand ideas that won't work," she spurted out in frustration as she turned towards another dead end. "Ugh, we're barely in this maze, and at this rate, it'll take us a whole hour to solve it,"

"Listen!" Hemsley whisper-shouted.

"What?" she whisper-shouted back.

"Let's go back to the entrance, and you hide by the employee's gate. I'll make a scene to distract the guards. Once they come after me, I'll make a dash towards the stables. When the guards leave the door, you simply walk right in," he said.

"But when you get caught without wearing a costume, they'll pummel you," she said.

"Bixby, really? So smart, and missing the obvious... I'm a ghost, remember? As soon as I get into the stables, I will keep them occupied for as long as I can and then when my back is against the wall I will simply disappear," he said.

For a second, Bixby could have kissed his nerdy forehead.

"Clever boy," she said as they dashed towards the entrance.

"Same rules as before: if you unlaunch, clear it with me before you try to launch back in," Bixby said before Hemsley's big moment.

"Hey! Over here!" he shouted, popping out into the open for the guards to see. "You two guys know where I can find a bunch of rich people to harass?"

"What the—"

Hemsley didn't wait for him to finish and took off for the stables with the pair of guards hot on his heels. A few seconds later, Bixby peeked around the corner to make sure the coast was clear. She was lucky that she didn't just dash for the door, because three more men in white burst out of the staff door in pursuit.

Bixby slid along the bushes so that the lookouts up on the ridge couldn't see her. She managed to catch the closing door and slip inside. She found herself standing inside a storage shed that held cleaning supplies, water filtration kits, and extra patio furniture. When she reached the door on the opposite side of the room, she cracked it open, and what she saw was stunning.

In the moonlight, the water falling from the snow cap above was glowing almost the same color as the glow worms back in Level One. It was a beautiful aquamarine that shimmered in the moonlight as it fell. The owner had made the pond into a pool for guests with patio furniture, a barbeque grill, and even a kiddy pool. It then ran off the side and down into a cavern that Bixby figured must go under the castle and out the front.

"I hope Harvey can duplicate this, too," she said to herself as she snuck out the door.

She continued creeping around the edge of the pool in slow increments depending on whether the guard was overlooking the pool or the stables. Right now, he was occupied by Hemsley running around in circles outside of the stables trying not to get caught.

Once she reached the waterfall base, she could see no possible way for her to be able to read anything on the wall as the cascade of ice-cold water crashed hard down on the side of the mountain face. This was Bixby's first real dead end. She sat for a moment, panicked, because if there was a clue, it would be impossible to get to without getting drenched.

"Think, Bixby. What are we missing?" she asked herself. "If it isn't obvious on this one then there has to be another way... unless..."

She slid back against the wall and made her way over to where the water dropped into the pool and disappeared over the infinity edge.

"Bingo," she said, looking down a flight of hidden stairs.

Bixby waited a moment to make sure the guard wasn't looking and then she slithered over the edge and down to the treads that led below ground. There was a hallway that followed alongside the river, and Bixby hurried beside the crashing water. First, she entered a room with generators and large filters. Bixby could only imagine that this was how they processed the water and pushed it into the castle. She had no time to admire the system because of the time crunch, so she pushed on. She followed the water that rushed through illuminated pipes. Her best guess was that the tunnel would lead under the balcony and then over the cliff.

Tipton would be fascinated with all of this engineering stuff, Bixby thought as she continued to run faster and faster. Through a set of double doors, she could see two rooms; one was marked "FURNACE ROOM" and the other was to the "VIEWING DECK." Bixby knew she had to get to the viewing deck, but she could hear a familiar whistling from the furnace room that was too enticing not to take a small peek.

"Where have I heard that before?" she asked herself as she slowly tried to open the door. But as she pulled, the hinges creaked loudly. She froze as the whistling stopped.

The plan was to run if she heard footsteps, but none came. After an eternity standing like a statue in the darkness, Bixby heard a low grumbly voice mutter some gibberish, and then the whistling returned.

Bixby sighed with relief. She then painstakingly moved with ninja silence as she backed away and turned towards the viewing deck.

Bixby couldn't believe how amazing it all was; she must have been standing right below the patio with the party going on above. There was a picture window that spanned the wall while the sounds of powerful waves filled the air. In the middle of that window, written in large letters, was the next riddle:

> *At the sound of me, some may recall a memory*
> *or even move their feet.*
> *At the sound of me, some may act foolish*
> *or even make them weep.*

Bixby quickly took out her card and jotted down the answer as she stuffed the paper back in her pocket. Taking a moment to look out at the water, she reached her hand around the glass and felt the cool mist on her palm. The rock ledge must have been only a few feet below the rail of the balcony.

"Bixby! I've got eight of them chasing me," Hemsley cried out over her earpiece, panting the entire time. "Now would be a good time to find some cover because I'm going to need to unlaunch here soon!"

Before she could reply, Tipton chimed in as well. "I'm going to need some help, too," he said. "And—Ow! Quit it!"

Bixby froze. "Tipton? What's going on?"

A pause settled before a new voice joined in, one that sent shivers down Bixby's spine.

"Hello, Bixby. Remember me?"

Tipton's Tako earring must have been removed from his ear. She took a breath knowing that this moment was inevitable.

"Leave him alone, Maggie. He has nothing to do with this," Bixby replied.

"I was a little uncertain if he would take the bait, but I'll give it to him. He's loyal and brave to climb out on the spire to come to help you," she said.

If Tipton didn't see her coming, she must have snuck up on him through the tunnel behind the dance panel. Either way, Maggie currently had the upper hand.

"What do you want from me, Maggie?" Bixby asked.

"You, of course," she hissed.

"Then you let him go back into the ballroom?"

"Absolutely."

"Alright. Where?" Bixby wanted logistics.

"Right here on the balcony. Look for Penny and Barnaby," she said. "Oh, and don't take too long. I'm impatient, and the drop from here is a long way down."

Bixby knew she was probably right below them on the balcony. "I'm on my way."

The line squelched with feedback and then went dead. Maggie must have smashed Tipton's Tako.

"Time for the second half of the plan," Bixby said once the line had cut out.

"On it," Hemsley shouted before he, too, went silent.

"Pippa, I hope you get back soon," she said into the roaring waterfall. "I'm going to need you before this is all over."

Chapter 20
Cat and Mouse

The fastest way back into the party was to get caught. Bixby knew that the men in white got paid extra if they caught a guest outside of the party, so instead of trying to lead them on a chase, it was easier to walk right up to them, and they would escort a rogue guest back to the ballroom. It was a risky move because, according to the guard's captain, getting caught a second time meant disqualification.

They took Bixby quickly once she presented herself and brought her through the main doors. Once inside, they handed her off to another man who seemed as if he were the one in charge of it all.

"Really? Another one got out?" the captain grumbled. He then leveled a stern finger at Bixby. "This is your only warning. We catch you again, and you're done. Understand?"

Bixby gave a simple nod.

"Good," he said. "Now get back in and stay."

She complied and quickly saw that Tipton was right. The party was vastly different from when they first arrived. Before, the dance floor was the place to be, and everyone was having a great time. Now the outer edges were lined with people formulating ideas as to the meaning of the Phantom's Riddle while there was still another much larger group that was still dancing the night away.

Sticking to the outer rim and trying to listen to people's theories, Bixby felt sad for them. Not a single person was anywhere close to answering the Phantom's Riddle. She also remembered when her grandfather first started giving her riddles; it took her forever to unlock the first step. She was grateful for all the time he had poured into her.

There was one stop at the DJ booth that needed to happen before she stepped into Maggie's trap. It took a few seconds to get DJ Doom's attention because he was busy conducting the party while surrounded by people and guards.

Bixby was hopeful that once Doom found out later that he was throwing the Level Two party, she could get him to do her actual Holo-School Prime dance. Bixby would probably go if he was performing.

Moving around the outside edge of it all, Bixby whispered to one of DJ Doom's security guards who then relayed her words to the entertainer. Apparently, it was enough for DJ Doom to take note of her.

"What can I do for you little lady?" he shouted over a deep bass groove.

"Do you let people sing?" Bixby's voice shouted back.

"Sorry, I don't do karaoke, but I can get you an autograph," he shouted back, reaching for a preprinted picture of him in his signature mask.

"No, that's okay. I just wanted to say my date is extremely famous like you. Thought maybe you would want to do live collaboration."

"Do you know how many times I've heard that? But I'll humor you tonight because this place is insane! The deal is, you tell me who it is, and I would consider it," he said, his words nearly drowned by the volume of the music.

"I can't give his name," Bixby countered. "You know, scavenger hunt rules and all. But he's got multiple platinum records. Promise."

"No name. No go," he replied as the song started to wind down. "Hold up, let me switch this beat." He stepped away from her and yelled out to the crowd as the music volume went low. His voice deepened. "Let me see you go side to side like this," he said as he swayed. "Build it up with me," he shouted to the crowd as he turned knobs furiously, and the song started to elevate. "Side-to-side," he kept building them up. "Let's go!" he shouted as he smashed the song's drop, and the crowd lost its mind.

He looked back at her with his mask's eyebrows raised and his head tilted a few degrees as if he were saying, "Name?"

She flagged DJ Doom back over, and shouted over the crowd and the music, "You're going to want to play 'Red Looks Best On Her' by Global Anarchy."

"Is that a fact?" DJ Doom asked.

"Yep," she said. "I'll go get him. He gets a little nervous sometimes, but no biggie."

Tipton was a spitting image, body build wise, to the up-and-coming hip-hop artist. Lucky for Tipton the masks helped hide the fact that he looked nothing like Global Anarchy when it came to his face.

"I think we all do when we first become stars," he said. "Green Suit that matches your dress?" She nodded, and he nodded back. "Alright. Let's do it. By the way, your mask is glitching; your mouth isn't moving."

There were a lot of things that were glitching for Bixby tonight so she said the first thing that came to her mind. "I accidentally got water all over it."

With another nod, he climbed back into the DJ perch and danced along with the crowd.

Before turning to make her next move, she caught a brief glimpse of a firework symbol on a crate stuffed under the DJ booth. She didn't have time to think about it now. For her it was time to square off with the last person she expected to be competing against.

It was a straight line over to the balcony from where she was backstage, but it took her forever in her mind to make the trip.

"Welcome back, Timmons," Barnaby said as she strolled up to the two brutes that made sure that Maggie and Tipton were not interrupted.

Bixby reached up, rubbed her nose, and gave him a smug half-smile, "You've got a little brown spot right here."

"Real cute," Penny replied for him.

"End of the line," Barnaby said stepping aside and letting Bixby go past.

Maggie's eyes lit up and she gushed. "Bixby!"

Bixby didn't reply.

"I have to hand it to you," Maggie said. "I was certain that those two would stall you long enough to make sure you didn't get more than two or three riddles, but bravo to you for getting as far as you did."

"You said you would let him…" Bixby had to choose her next words carefully because Tipton was currently being held against the railing. If she said "let him go," there would be a chance it meant over the rail similar to what she tried to do to Bixby in the last level.

Maggie caught onto the hesitation.

"Now Bixby, you don't think I would do something awful to Tipton do you? I made a promise, and I intend to keep it," she said holding his lapel tightly. He looked petrified.

"I would never go back on my promise, and now that you are here with me, Tipton can go back to the ballroom," she said.

A pause settled, and Bixby couldn't tell if it was disbelief by Tipton or terror had him slow to move, but before he did, she pointed to the spire, "… via the spire."

"That wasn't part of the deal," Bixby growled.

"You said to let him go back to the ballroom. You didn't say by what means," she said. "Now get going before I change my mind."

Before Tipton had a chance to process what was going on, there was a commotion outside of the hedge line. "He had better get out here soon, or it's a no go!" someone called.

Bixby straightened and shouted back. "We're over here!"

Two guys suddenly appeared from around the corner, part of DJ Doom's security, and easily pushed their way through Penny and Barnaby.

"This guy?" they asked, pointing to Tipton.

Bixby nodded excitedly. "Yeah. That's him!"

Immediately, the guards waved at Tipton. "Move it. You're on in two."

Bixby could see that Maggie was starting to boil at the counter trick Bixby had pulled.

Letting go of his coat, Tipton straightened up his jacket and walked towards Bixby, stopping in front of her.

"These two gentlemen are with DJ Doom and are here to escort you to the stage for your performance with him," Bixby said with a smile.

"My... My performance?" he asked.

"'Red Looks Best On Her' is the one you will be leading off with, and then see how the night goes," Bixby replied.

"If you're not at the stage in one minute, you can forget about it," one of the guards tacked on.

"And I'm sure they will let you stay backstage with these guys for the rest of the Riddle, too," Bixby said, bobbing her head toward the two from security.

Tipton cocked his head. "Why am I going backstage with them, exactly?"

"So you can stay safe," Bixby said.

"But I won't be able to help," he countered.

"You being safe is more important."

For a moment, it looked like Tipton was about to go along with it, but he stopped the moment he began as a new thought dawned on him. "So...wait," he stammered. "You never really were letting me help to begin with? I mean, not really help..."

Tipton's sudden realization caught Bixby so off guard she was at a loss for words.

Her friend furrowed his brow.

Maggie clapped. "Oh, Bixby. Bravo," she said. "I thought I was cold hearted, but he doesn't know that you have been leaving him in the ballroom all night so you can solve the Riddle by yourself?"

Tipton didn't seem to hear her, as he stammered on, trying to wrap his head around it all. "You...you didn't think I could actually do anything?"

"No, that's not it at all," Bixby said, reeling at what to say next because it was exactly what she had been doing all night.

"This could *not* have gone any better," Maggie cackled as she looked at her teammates in disbelief. "At least you two knew that you were pawns. Poor Tippy here actually thought he was doing something useful."

One of the guards grunted. "Look, are you coming or not?" he said with a snort. "I don't care either way, but I've got to tell Doom something."

Tipton's face turned bright red. "Nope!" he said, stomping his foot. "I'm not going to do a song and dance for you, and I'm certainly not going to be anyone's stupid bargaining chip."

The guards shrugged and walked back towards the ballroom.

With that, Tipton jumped up on the rock railing, pressed against the spire, and reached out for his first foothold.

"Tipton, no!" Bixby cried.

"You heard the man," Maggie said, holding out her hand and stepping in Bixby's path. "He doesn't want you around anymore."

Bixby wilted as she saw how crushed Tipton was.

"Time to head back to the cave and take that seat," Barnaby said with a devilish grin.

Penny shot a grin of her own and circled around Bixby. "Let's go. Nice and easy."

Maggie, too, closed in. "It'll be good for you to have a nice, quiet place to cry it out."

They had made sure that Bixby had absolutely no escape except into the arms of one of the three of them.

If it were not for Tipton's epiphany, the trap part of Bixby's plan had worked perfectly.

Bixby made sure Hemsley stepped into the silver light of moon and instructed him to look right at Maggie before she spoke, "Joke's on you: Tipton might not be safe with the guards and really mad at me right now, but I wish I could see the look on your pretty little mask when you realize you just let your bargaining chip get away with nothing to show for it," Bixby mocked through the motionless dark red lips of the hologram that stood before Maggie.

"Wait...What?" Penny said confused.

"Is that a hologram of Bixby? How'd she get a hologram into..." Barnaby's sentence trailed off

"Now this is embarrassing," Hemsley said as the lips of the hologram started moving when he spoke. Even in the uncertainty, he stayed the course of the plan.

"You really should be here, Bixby. I think her head might *actually* explode," he snarked some more.

Behind Maggie, Hemsley could see that Penny and Barnaby were slowly backing away, most likely out of fear.

"Timmons," Maggie hissed in a low voice, pulling close to Hemsley's hologram that was overlayed with the image of Bixby in her dress and mask. "I know you can hear me."

Another long pause followed. "When I find you, I'm going to make sure you have to drink those stupid turkey sandwiches through a straw for the rest of your life."

Her words came out slow and cold, but with what Bixby was certain was terrible truth.

"You'd be scary if last place didn't look so good on you," Bixby said with a smirk, knowing it would set her off.

Maggie uselessly ripped at the holographic body Hemsley was controlling.

Bixby was relieved that Pippa was able to create the holographic hack earlier in the night, but she was growing more and more concerned that Pippa, like her parents, had gone completely silent and Tipton furious with her while hanging off the side of the castle. Just when she was going to utilize her team to full capacity, her team was slowly withering.

Right before Hemsley unlaunched, Maggie said the words that made Bixby's heart sink so fast that she almost threw up.

"Follow him up that spire. He doesn't make it to the window."

CHAPTER 21
EVEN-ISH

Tucked neatly in the back corner of the viewing room, Bixby gave up on Level Two of the Riddle. Though she had a brief moment of hesitation, there was only one real choice: save her best friend.

With no communication, Bixby had to run as hard as she could if she was going to reach Tipton in time.

Through the tunnels she sprinted, gliding around each bend at breakneck speed. The goal was to get to the house and jump into the window that was closest to the spiral staircase. From there she could scale the inside of the spire and meet him at the window, or climb down to get him, whatever was needed.

Up through the pool room she came, bounding up each step and hopping over the lawn chairs that were laid out. Her shoulder hit the first door as she eyed the next door that would dump out at the employee's entrance. The second door, however, met her with a thud and a sore shoulder.

"Oaf!" she and someone else shouted simultaneously as Bixby fell to the ground with the wind nearly knocked out of her chest.

"What was that?" a deep voice shouted from the now half open door.

Bixby looked up and could see two guards push the entry the rest of the way open, while another one was sprawled out on the ground like her.

"It's that girl we caught before," one of the men replied.

The second guard grinned. "Bonus pay. Grab her!"

Bixby's mind went into puzzle-solving overdrive. If she were caught a second time, she wouldn't be able to help Tipton, and this path to Tipton was no longer an option. A guard reached down to grab her as a plan solidified in her head.

"Not today boys," Bixby said, yanking a trash can filled with yard tools down between her and her potential captors to delay their pursuit. The mess gave her enough time to push up off the ground back towards the pool deck.

It was pulling the lawn chairs that were stacked by the door that she had to time precisely right after she slammed the pool deck door in the guard's face. It was more of an inconvenience to the men in white to climb over the chairs, but it gave Bixby enough time to get over the pool's edge and back down onto the hidden stairwell.

"She went down there!" she heard the guard from up on a ledge cry out.

Bixby sprinted through the filtration room as the water flowed through the glowing tube above her. It wasn't easy. The one thing Cody hadn't thought about was that wearing dress shoes and a fancy gown while competing in the Level was very inconvenient. For what she was about to do next, the dress shoes she had on were unnecessary.

The guards had made up much of the distance between them as she reached the furnace and viewing room doors.

Bixby sprang through the door in the viewing room, flicked her feet, and off came her slip-ons. She dashed towards the open glass next to the falls and climbed up on the edge right as the guards burst in the door. The gap was narrow enough that she could barely shimmy through.

"Come on now, don't do anything stupid ma'am," the guard said, seeing her inch over the ledge.

"Move and I jump, and I will make sure I scream loud enough that everyone on the balcony can hear," Bixby threatened.

The other guard inched closer, hands up defensively. "Hey now, we don't need to do anything rash."

Bixby was scoping out some hand holds that she could grab onto, and the closest one was about four feet from the ledge. She would have to jump to reach the grip. It was the only way.

"Here goes nothing," she muttered right as she took the leap.

The guards went into a shouting frenzy, but she paid them no heed now that she had a firm grip on the lip of the rock. Unfortunately, the grip turned out to be slipperier than expected. Worse, she couldn't find another hold nearby.

One of the guards leaned out and offered her a hand. "Take it!"

She didn't. Instead, her gaze drifted to the balcony ledge above, not even three feet away. If she could get there, she'd be safe. Key word: if.

"Man, I really didn't think this one through very well," she said to herself as she struggled to hold on. Bixby looked down at the gorge below as her grip weakened and then failed altogether.

But she didn't fall.

In fact, she went up.

"You're going to need to be more careful, Timmons," Marin's voice rang out over the sound of the falls, her hand firmly grasping Bixby's wrist before giving her a tug towards safety.

Bixby was now standing on the balcony, damp but safe. For a split second, she was sure she was going to take the twenty-second plunge down to the bottom of the cliff to her certain doom.

"How did you..." she stammered, brushing herself off.

"You're not the only one trying to find a riddle behind a waterfall. The boys said there was nothing out in the garden, so this was the next logical place," she said. "The guards shouting helped, too."

"Good thinking," Bixby said, rubbing her sore hands. "I'd chat more, but I've got to get to Tipton."

Bixby started to move, but Marin cleared her throat and froze her in place. "You don't want to go that way," she said.

"Why not?" Bixby ask curiously.

"Because Tipton made it to the top and started chucking things out the window at Maggie and her team. I guess that gave him enough time to race down to the bottom of the stairs and tie the doorhandle to the hutch outside. They're on their way back down the spire right now."

Bixby couldn't help but to smile. Tipton not only beat them up the spire, but he also used their own trick against them.

"So, we're stuck in the ballroom then?" Bixby asked, less concerned about Maggie and more concerned about not being able to get to Tipton and apologize.

"I'm going to get in trouble for this, but the other spire is climbable and dumps out on the second floor. It's a more difficult climb, but it gets you out of the ballroom," Marin said, pointing to the other tower.

"Come with me," Bixby urged.

"Na, I'll wait until they get back down here and hold them off for you long enough for you to grab the next clue up there and get to your friend," Marin said with a smile, eyes a little misty.

"Thank you," Bixby said.

"Thank me when we are both in the next level," Marin quipped.

Bixby nodded. "FYI, the answer to the waterfalls is 'music.'"

"Perfect. Thanks," she said, walking away. "And good luck."

With that, Bixby took off thinking it was nice to know the teams were officially a bit more even now.

"It is like a never-ending sprint up a wall," Bixby said as she made her way over to the base of the second summit.

As she got there, she heard Hemsley call out to her. "Hey! You're okay!"

"Yeah. What happened to you?" Bixby asked, grabbing the first-hand hold sounding a little sassy.

"I tried to randomly launch in to freak the guards out, but your earring was moving fast, and I couldn't lock on to your signal. Were you running?" he asked.

"You could say that," she said as she locked into her climb.

"Do you want me to log out and log back in once you make it to the top?" Hemsley asked.

"No, I need you here to let me know what's happening in the ballroom, including if you can see where the fire started."

Hemsley frowned and his brow furloughed. "So, Tipton really left the team?"

"You saw what happened on the balcony. I hate to break it to you, but Pippa isn't patching through. There are no communications with Pinnacle Manor. Maggie crushed Tipton's earpiece, and he's somewhere loose in the castle. For now, you're the only one left on team Timmons until I can make things right with Tipton," she said as she pulled herself further into the night sky.

"Okay, but we don't have a lot of time."

"I can solve along the way if something pops up, but crossing the finish-line alone isn't worth whatever Cody has to offer," Bixby said, pushing harder up the wall thinking of how mad Tipton must be.

"I'll do my best to blend in. I really hope he listens," he said, pausing between thoughts before heading for the hedges to spy on the party.

Finding hidden puzzles with a fire supposedly starting at any random time was stressful enough, but the thought of not reaching Tipton before time was up made Bixby's climb more desperate, and even a bit clumsy as she went. Aside from the two slips when she tried hurrying her climb, it didn't take Bixby long to scale the spire. It took her even less time to see the next clue that Marin said would be in the room. On the floor opposite the window was a sprawled-out bear rug sitting right in front of a fireplace with a reading chair on top of it. Bixby flung herself in the window and searched under the chair and the rug.

"Nothing," she said as she moved the chair and flipped the bear rug over. Even its underside had nothing on it.

"I am sure this is '*under the gargantuan omnivore*,'" Bixby said wrestling with where the riddle could be. She lifted its head and looked into the bear's mouth, but all she saw was a bunch of shiny, sharp, white teeth.

I'm wasting time. I've got to get to Tipton, Bixby thought, turning to leave the clue hunt alone. She let the head drop to the ground with a hollow *THUNK*.

Stopping at the sound of the noise, she again jammed her hands in the bear's mouth. This time she pulled it out of the way with all of her might. Cut in the floor, she saw a small hole big enough for just one finger. "I hope there isn't anything on the other side of that hole that bites," she said as she wedged her pinky finger inside and tugged. The floorboard was loose and flipped up on a hinge. Underneath the slate was carved another riddle.

You Wait for it.
You See It.
You hear it.
It's Gone.

Bixby pulled out her pad knowing that the answer to this riddle was something that she'd seen over and over in this Level.

She quickly jotted the answer and sprinted down the spiral staircase that let out on the second floor. Bixby had to find a way down to the first floor to see if she could catch up with Tipton. Her only option at the moment was the staircase that was being watched by two guards.

"Can't go that way," she said to herself scanning the hallway.

She thought, spotting massive cords that were holding back silky curtains framing a painting at the end of the hall. Without concern for running into any of her competitors, Bixby began another all-out sprint. In her mind she was thanking herself for sticking to her daily workouts, because even though she was tired, she felt better than in Level One.

With a yank of the cord, the drapery around a painting of a medieval queen let loose. Bixby pulled the second cord and started to tie them together while using her elbow to push open the closest bedroom door. Pulling the knot tight, she froze in her tracks.

I've spent all night trying to find riddles, and now when I'm trying to get to Tipton, they keep distracting me, she thought racing to the bed rail to tie off her rope.

The walls were covered in floral prints. The carpet was bright red with floral designs, and the bedspread was covered in flower petals. Bixby had no doubt that this was going to be the answer to the "roses love ash" riddle. The problem was that there was no time to test each of the flowerpots to see which one held the next clue.

Bixby had a devious idea. The entire house was going to burn down sometime tonight anyway, so what did it matter if the room got a little dirty? She ran to the fireplace and made sure the ashes were cool; she didn't want to be the person to start the Shadow Deep blaze. They were bone dry. So, she went over to the fireplace tools and grabbed the shovel. With a big heave, she took the biggest scoop she could, turned around, and threw it all over the room. Ashes covered the dresser and all the flowers on it with this scoop. Nothing budged. She then repeated it on the reading chair with the same result. Next, she tossed a big pile against the picture of roses above the fireplace that rained down on the roses on the mantle. Still, nothing moved.

"One last place to look," she said with a grin as she turned towards the beautiful bed covered with rose petals. With a sweeping motion over the entire bed, Bixby covered it in ashes. The rose petals looked as if they instantly withered under their cover, and a mist rose from the bedspread. The clue was written out in ash hovering over the covers.

It's a dangerous place where you can get burned, cut, or even cooked alive;
It's also the place where vittles hide.

Lucky for Bixby, Miss Marmalade is a lady with good southern vocabulary, because Bixby knew exactly what vittles were. She didn't pull out her paper knowing she could remember this answer.

A second later, the floor rumbled under Bixby's feet and the immediate sounds of screams came from the hallway: something had exploded.

CHAPTER 22
THE SIDE GAME

The whole house groaned as Bixby made her way to the doorway.

"Hemsley!" Bixby shouted in panic. There was no response for a few agonizing seconds as she peeked out.

"Bixby, are you okay?" Hemsley said over the intercom.

"I'm on the second floor. What happened?" Bixby asked, hearing screaming coming from the stairwell.

Hemsley's voice began to break up, and it didn't seem like he could hear her anymore. "Bixby? Are you there? You're cutting out!"

"Hemsley?" she asked through the crackle of the Tako. Bixby continued to try and make the connection work, but for some reason, she could only hear him.

"Bixby, if you can hear me, you have to get to the ballroom. It's in flames. I don't know where Tipton is either!" he was shouting over people yelling to go up the stairs. "I have no clue how it started either!"

His transmission cut off, and now he was gone along with Pippa and her family. Tipton was all Bixby had left at the moment, and she really didn't have him, either.

Bixby began barreling towards the staircase in the middle of Shadow Deep. She could hear the growing bellows of the guards' shouting directions at guests as they filed out.

BEEP-BEEP, BEEP-BEEP!

Bixby's Tako earring was trying to pair with something.

"Barnaby," she realized she hadn't used Pippa's hack to spy on him yet. Now was as good a time as any to reach up and connect. Bixby's eyes shifted down to the stairwell to the carpet below her. "He must be standing on the landing above the dance floor," she calculated where he could be within fifty feet as she accepted the Bluetooth pair.

"That moron got caught two seconds into the castle, and the guards put him right back into our hands. I made sure he won't be bothered in the bathroom," he sneered as Bixby began her eavesdrop.

"And we made sure Marin stays there as well," she heard Wesley say. "But we couldn't find her answer sheet. Did she give them to you?"

"She gave me the last two answers. We have everything, and Bixby has nothing, including her friends" Barnaby replied.

"Except a reason not to bury you both," Bixby chimed in with searing heat in her voice.

"Bixby! How long have you been..."

Not giving him the satisfaction of demanding an answer, she had already hung up the call.

Barnaby, in his orange costume, spun around and could see Bixby making her way down the stairwell towards him. Panicked at her approach, he dashed for the exit.

"Bixby!" Hemsley shouted from across the hall.

Bixby met him at the foot of the stairs.

"I couldn't get you on your earrings," he said as they met at the bottom of the steps with people rushing by them to exit the castle.

"I have to find Tipton and Marin. They're still in the ballroom," she said.

"How do you know?"

"Tell you later!" she shouted as she raced for the grand staircase.

Against a sea of party guests, Bixby stayed close behind Hemsley as people parted for the hologram. Bixby pushed aside anyone who happened to glance through him. The duo was heading right into the inferno.

Guards were waving people up the ballroom stairs as Bixby and Hemsley reached the railing where she'd been announced as an honored guest earlier that night.

"You can't go down there," the concierge said.

Hemsley didn't hesitate to dash in the opposite direction of the steps as a decoy. A man in white jumped to grab Hemsley, but he grasped thin air and tumbled to the ground, baffled.

"Ghost," he said, chuckling as he pointed to himself proudly.

Looking up from the floor, the man could see Bixby darting towards the ballroom entrance. "Stop! It's too dangerous!"

Bixby continued her run.

The dance floor was completely cleared out as Bixby scanned the room. Whatever made the explosion had shattered the glass of every window and mirror. She knew where Barnaby said Tipton was, but a quick scan confirmed that neither Tipton or Marin was in the ballroom.

Great, they probably tied him to a toilet, Bixby thought as she made her way past the buffet table.

Bixby had no doubt that the men's room was probably empty when she burst through the door. Much to her surprise, a boy in a rainbow suit was at the sink washing his hands.

"Don't you realize that this place is on fire?" she shouted.

"I know! This is an awesome party, right? The bass on that system shook the whole—" he started.

"No! This place is *REALLY* on fire!" she shouted, holding the door open to expose the flames behind her.

The boy's eyes nearly burst out of his head at the sight of the firestorm.

"Don't just stand there. MOVE!" she screamed.

It didn't take much convincing; the boy raced towards her.

"Oh, there's some dude in one of the stalls getting sick," he said as he made his way past her.

"Tipton?" she said.

From inside a stall, she could hear a muffled voice trying to scream. Bixby could understand why the boy would have confused it for barfing.

She went to the only closed door and insisted, "Stand back!"

With all of her might, Bixby threw her shoulder into the door several times. On the fifth ram, the latch snapped, and the door flung open revealing Tipton tied to a toilet. His mouth was gagged with a strip of thick cloth.

"Looks like you could use a little help," she said as she started to pull on the knots of the rope.

He nodded furiously.

"Let me guess; six-foot-tall, orange suit?" she asked as she continued to free him. "Listen, Tipton. I'm really sorry for not letting you help me in the riddle more. I just wanted to keep you safe. I didn't mean—" she started, but Tipton pulled the tie from his mouth interrupting her. "Did you see the look on Maggie's face when I yelled at her!" he said laughing.

"What's so funny? You yelled at me, too" Bixby replied.

"Wait, you didn't think I meant any of that did you, Bixby?"

Bixby bashfully pulled on the last knot realizing Tipton had duped her also.

"Listen, Bixby, I know you close up when things get stressful and say things you don't mean," he started as he helped try to wriggle the rope free. "But I figured the best way to help you was for you to tell me what you needed me to do, and I did it. I thought you were giving me the option of taking the safe route with DJ Doom or helping you keep Penny, Barnaby, and Maggie off your back, so I improvised, which I am getting really good at, and I let them chase me up the wall."

"You could have been really hurt," Bixby replied.

"I know, right? Very fun, but I would not like to do that again," he said as the last knot let loose.

"Then you're not mad at me?" she asked, confirming the new revelation.

"Not a chance on your life! This has been the greatest thing that has ever happened to me!" he replied.

Bixby didn't know what to say. Tipton was indeed her very best friend, and awkwardly in a bathroom stall, she gave him the biggest hug she could.

"Thank you, Tipton," she said with another tear welling in her eye. Bixby never liked being sentimental, but her heart was racing knowing Tipton didn't hate her.

"Thank me when we get out of this fire and have won this level," he said, giving her a squeeze.

Bixby propped open the doors, and the heat from the flames was getting exponentially more intense.

"Did you see what started the fire?" she asked.

"No, I was a bit tied up when I heard the boom," Tipton replied as they made their way down the bathroom corridor. "Sorry I got caught. I tied the spire door shut, but then when Maggie started pounding on the door, I stayed longer than I should've to egg her on. I was having so much fun taunting her that I didn't see the guard walk up behind me."

Bixby shook her head. "No need to apologize," she said realizing that Tipton was more help than she knew. As the blaze drew nearer Bixby refocused on the task at hand, "We have to find Marin."

Their dash towards the ballroom came to a screeching halt when a masked figure backlit by fire made their way up the bathroom stairs.

"There you are, Timmons, and your pudgy friend too!"

If voices were spiders, Mad Maggie's would be the biggest, toothiest, and hairiest one that Bixby could think of.

Flanking Maggie was Penny and Barnaby; neither of them seemed excited to be standing near a growing fire.

"You going to let this place fall on all of us, Maggie?" Bixby said, smirking.

"Oh no, Bixby. I'm going to wait until the last possible minute, and then walk out the front door," Maggie replied as she barricaded Bixby and Tipton in the hallway.

Bixby and Tipton were outnumbered and in a position with no other way out besides through the trio. Maggie had the upper hand.

"You win, Maggie. We don't have all the riddles, so let's go outside together and you can keep us there," Bixby said.

A moment later, the DJ booth crumpled under the weakened structure.

"I have to hand it to you, Bixby; that move you made on the balcony with the hologram was brilliant," Maggie said with a nod. "And for a second, I thought Tipton was more than a dopey sidekick."

"He has nothing to do with us, but I'm here now, and I don't plan to stay long," Bixby said steadying her stance that Marin taught her.

Tipton shirked a bit behind her hoping Bixby wouldn't do anything rash.

Maggie could sense Bixby was ready to fight her way past but didn't show that she cared to engage.

"Can't do that, Timmons. My instructions are to make sure you don't have a chance to find any more clues before this place goes up," she said while surveying the ongoing destruction.

"There aren't any roses in here, and none of the horses in the stables were dark," Bixby said, hoping she could bluff which two riddles she didn't have.

Barnaby tapped Maggie on the shoulder, and wrinkles formed across his brow. "Uh...the carpet on the stairs is burning."

Maggie briefly twisted to throw the stairs a glance. "We only need a few more seconds," she said, shrugging. She then looked down at Bixby's feet and grinned. "Tough break losing your shoes."

"Yeah, well, I say we get going," Barnaby said, tugging on her shoulder again. "This is good enough."

"He's right," Penny said. "Let's go."

Maggie sized up the inferno one last time before nodding. "Alright. We can go. But we're taking Tipton with us."

Tipton retreated and balled his fists. "No way. I'm staying with Bixby."

Bixby reached back and grabbed his wrist. "I'll be fine. Go."

"But—"

Bixby spun and gave him a hug. "Go," she said loud enough for the others to hear. Her follow up words were then whispered close to his ear. "I still need to get Marin, which means you need to give them the slip and continue to solve the riddle out there, partner."

At that point, Bixby let him go. He saw her hand slip from inside his inner jacket pocket in the process. Parting with her answer sheet was the biggest gesture of trust she could think of. He held the future of Bixby's Cody chase in a small pocket inside his lapel.

"I mean it," Bixby said, growling this time. "Get out of here!"

Tipton enjoyed her theatrics and bashfully nodded, playing along.

Ceiling tiles fell, crashing down behind everyone and causing them all to jump. A split second later, Tipton rushed toward the steps, covering his face. The flames were almost unbearable now.

He held his back against the marble wall furthest from Maggie as he made his way out of the hallway. She gave a little jump towards him, and he nearly broke out into a run around her right into Barnaby's watchful care. Bixby wasn't sure if he was really scared of Maggie this time or playing the part. She opted to believe in the latter.

Once Penny and Barnaby were gone with their captive, Bixby felt more in control.

"I don't like fighting, Bixby," Maggie said.

"You didn't seem to have a problem with it on the side of the mountain in the last Level," Bixby said, still searching for a way out.

"I am sorry; that was a misleading statement. I don't like to fight, but that doesn't mean I won't," she said with a smile. "It brings out the worst in both people, and as an artist at heart, I don't like to mess up my hands."

"You knew I was helping you and sincere about getting out of Level One together: why did you jump ship?" Bixby asked, hoping to reach her on another level.

"You already know Marin was the original target, but you had to go and ruin it by becoming friends," Maggie replied. "But in the end, this was going to be your stop in the Riddle anyway, so I guess it never really mattered what happened last time."

A beam creaked above, and Maggie retreated a few steps so that she was at the top of the staircase. "Might want to watch that," she said, pointing.

Bixby did, and at the same time, she took a few steps toward the stairs, as well, thinking she might be able to make a run for it. Fear, however, kept her from doing such a thing.

Thankfully, because of her delay, she wasn't crushed by a beam that fell between the two girls a moment later, sending a show of sparks in all directions.

The fiery piece of wood angled sharply across the archway, wedged into place with large stones that rested above it. The collapse left the ground covered in hot coals and only provided a small opening in the lower left corner of the exit.

Bixby backed reflexively. Though the hole was likely big enough to squeeze through, it was filled with flames. Burning embers pelted her dress, and she quickly batted them away before retreating even more.

"Maybe we'll see you on the outside!" Maggie hollered from the other side. "Then again, maybe not!"

Chapter 23
The Next Crazy Move

Bixby was alone with nobody to rescue her this time. She desperately tried to think of her next move, but the floor was starting to be unbearable on her feet. She kept taking steps back to reach cooler tiles, but the smoke combined with the heat threatened to overwhelm her in a few more seconds.

Thinking of resources, Bixby's mind wandered back to the powder room and all the mirrors. The first part of her chaotic self-rescue rapidly came together.

"Shoes," she said, as she turned to run back into the mirror-laced room. The mannequins were dressed like the partygoers, complete with footwear.

Bixby plowed over the first one she saw with her shoulder. The purple-dressed dummy tore loose from its foundation, dislodging the mirror it was holding from its hands. With a great crash, the two of them smashed to the ground. She rolled off the tall, hard plastic body and pulled the shoes from its feet. Though they were a tad tight, Bixby didn't care. They provided much needed protection. She then noticed the cape the mannequin was wearing, and Bixby's next problem was solved.

Bixby's first thought had been to wriggle through the opening; however, the flames would burn her to a crisp before she even made it halfway through. With the cape in hand, she now had a new, more unorthodox plan.

Her jog had become another dash. In her mind, this was no different than sliding down the hill on a sheet of plastic covered in water and soap during the summer. In theory, it was doable. In practice, it was a stretch, but she was out of options.

When Bixby went head-first, clutching the makeshift sled, she glided along the tile much better than she had anticipated. The hole was narrow, and she had to hit it just right. She slammed into the wall thanks to a slight miscalculation, and ended up tucked tightly against it, eyes closed, fervently praying the shortest prayer she knew. "Please!"

Bixby kicked off the wall, trying to shoot for the hole once again. This time, she slid straight and true through the hole. The heat singed her hair and forced her to close her eyes. Then...then there was a sensation of nothing...

Bixby opened her eyes right as she cleared the top of the staircase and entered freefall. Her body sailed through the air and crashed on the last two marble steps on the way down. A new kind of pain wracked every part of her body that the floor touched.

She instinctively tucked in agony and crashed into the legs of the buffet. Pulling what was left of the shawl away from her face, she scampered as fast as she could out from under the table as it creaked and began to tip. The table fell right after she cleared it, sending charred food and drink across the floor.

Bixby stood and shook her head, exhaling sharply, both thrilled and exhausted she'd foiled yet another one of Maggie's traps. She was glad to be in one piece, but her dress was now far from being able to be salvaged.

But her work was far from done.

"Marin!" she called, looking left and right. "Marin, where are you?"

A coughing fit took hold, and Bixby knew she had to get fresh air, lest she pass out and succumb to the fire. With that, she raced for the balcony, and hoped along the way that perhaps she'd find Marin there, too.

Bixby sped across the ballroom floor. Flames consumed the DJ booth, and the mirror behind it was long since shattered, along with the windows for the balcony. Bixby bolted outside and headed for her previous hiding spot near the spire and cave door, looking and calling for Marin every step of the way.

There was no sign of her.

Bixby leaned over the railing and looked but still saw nothing. Then, out of the corner of her eye, she saw a shred of orange material on the ground near the second spire, by a potted plant. Instantly, Bixby hiked up what was left of her once beautiful green gown and sprinted towards the planter. Marin was propped up against the rail, overlooking the waterfall.

"Marin!" Bixby shouted, bolting over to her.

When she got there, Marin didn't respond. She didn't even move. Her mask was broken in three places with a whole section missing, exposing a gash on her cheek almost an inch wide. It had begun to rain, and the precipitation cascading down her mask mixed with blood from her cheek, and then down onto her orange dress.

Panicked, Bixby began patting the sides of her face. "Come on, Marin. Wake up!"

Marin groaned and lolled her head to one side. "Oh man. What happened?" she asked, looking around, dazed.

"The fire started, and we've got to get out of here. Can you stand?" Bixby asked.

"I think so."

Bixby took her arm and slung it over her shoulder.

Marin screamed in pain. "Stop! Stop!"

"What?" Bixby asked, trying to look her over for injuries.

"My leg!" she replied, grimacing. "I think it's broken."

Bixby exposed Marin's shine to assess the damage. Marin's leg was now covered in a huge bruise.

"Oh, Marin. Who did this to you?" Bixby asked assessing the damage.

"I don't know. One moment I'm on the balcony waiting for instructions, the next moment you're waking me up."

It didn't matter, she had it narrowed down to only a few suspects. Bixby was certain that there would be no way for her to carry Marin out by herself based on the extent of the injury. Bixby concluded that they were in serious danger.

"Somebody help us!" Bixby cried out over the growing sound of rain and the crumbling of the castle.

Marin tried to move again but failed. Tears welled in her eyes, and she shook her head as she accepted the seemingly inevitable. "I'm never going to make it out," she said, voice shaky.

"You're getting out if I have to drag you the whole way," Bixby said with determination.

Marin slumped back down against the rail. "No, you can't," Marin said. She then reached into a pocket and pulled out a crumpled piece of paper. "Take it. It has all the answers. You can use it to win."

Bixby shook her head. "Knock it off. I'm not leaving you."

"Yes, you are."

"No, I'm not!"

Bixby's eyes welled. She knew they were both in deep trouble and she couldn't see a way out of the inferno they could both take. The ballroom was impassable now, and the drop behind them over the falls would kill them without a doubt. The spires spewed fire, and the walls were beginning to crack. Bixby reasoned that if the flames didn't get them, the spires would soon crumble down on top of them. There was nothing left to do but maybe try to dodge the stones when they started to break free. Hope was in short supply as the rain was falling heavier now. It was still no match for the inferno that raged inside. Bixby stuffed the note into her pocket knowing that there was no longer any use for it now.

"Did you really mean that we could be sisters?" Marin asked as the two huddled against the rail together.

"Always wanted one," Bixby said as she hugged Marin.

As they sat there together, the wall opposite the DJ booth buckled first and let out a tremendous rumble as it toppled to the stone floor.

"We'll be okay," Bixby lied, closing her eyes and pulling Marin tight.

Then, from out of nowhere, someone shouted at them both.

"What are you two lunatics doing out here!"

CHAPTER 24
WELL HIDDEN

Bixby looked around frantically. Her heart was nearly beating out of her chest at the sound of the voice. In the distance, near the base of one of the spires and the wall of the ballroom, a head was sticking out of the ground.

"Daryl?" Bixby asked, thinking back to the familiar face she'd stared at so many times back home—the guy who set fireworks off in her cube.

Whoever it was, it didn't matter in the end because the soot-covered man was climbing out of the secret passage under the balcony floor and dashing toward them.

Bixby jumped up. "I think her leg is broken. I can't carry her."

The man looked over Marin before ripping a branch off a nearby tree. He then knelt next to the girl and splinted her leg, tying it with his handkerchief and a strip of Marin's torn orange dress hem.

"Not my best work, but it'll do," he said as he pulled Marin off the ground. "Let's get out of here."

Marin winced as he adjusted his grip on her, but because she was being rescued, she refused to complain as they took off.

"How did you find us?" Bixby asked.

"The doc who built this place didn't want guests to have to see us dirty workers, so he made a few tunnels so that we could come and go without bothering the company. I was simply looking to see if I could find out where that explosion came from, and there you were!"

"Where did it come from?" Bixby asked. "The furnace?"

"No, the furnace is running at tip-top shape," he replied as they traveled. "Not a thing wrong with it."

Bixby frowned, now not sure what had caused the fire. She kept quiet as she followed him down a platform, through some doors, and then through the water filtration system. They then hastily made their way through the long corridor to the landing below the pond area. The guards from earlier had returned to their post at the waterfalls.

"Howdy boys," Bixby said as the furnace man led them up the steps and around the water.

"Not you again," the first guard grumbled.

The second shrugged with a smirk. "More money for us."

"You do know the house is on fire, right?" she asked as they approached.

The first laughed and shook his head. "Nice try."

"You seriously can't hear it burning to the ground?"

"I'm sure it's just the fireworks."

"You two are really dense," Daryl replied, pushing past them and kicking open the door. "That's the biggest fireworks show to never leave the ground!"

The two guards made their way out of the shed and, for the first time, realized that the castle at Shadow Deep *was* on fire. The center of the structure was fully engulfed and was now working its way down the hallways in both directions.

Daryl pushed on, not bothering with the guards anymore, clearly looking for someone else. Bixby struggled to keep up. Nearing the stables, Bixby spied a woman wearing a white and silver dress. She didn't wear a face mask, and she was clearly in distress. The entire crowd was now watching her plea for help to a man dressed in a charcoal grey suit. She was certain that neither of them was at the party in the ballroom.

"You made it out!" Tipton shouted, rushing through the crowd and alongside Bixby and Marin.

"Thanks to Daryl," Bixby said, giving Tipton a quick hug of relief.

Tipton cocked his head. "The fireworks guy?"

"Yep," Bixby said. "How'd you get away from Penny and Barnaby?"

"Let's just say DJ Doom and his security team are good resources to have," he said with a grin.

Bixby helped prop Marin up in the stable, and once she was there, she pressed for the follow up. "Details, Tipton. Details."

"Well, as soon as we got near Doom's security guards and the guys in white, I started shouting, 'These two are the ones who started the fire!' and pointed to Penny and Barnaby."

Bixby raised her eyebrows, impressed. "They bought it?"

"Doom didn't believe me at first, but pushed it enough that he had them round up for questions," Tipton said, his smile now spanning from ear to ear. "Guess he decided us famous people have to stick together."

The conversation derailed as the woman in white entered a full meltdown, stealing everyone's attention.

"He's still inside!" she cried.

"There's nothing I can do," the man said sadly, shaking his head.

Whoever this guy was, he must have been who Daryl was looking for, because Daryl made a beeline for the man. "Doc!" he yelled. "This girl over here needs your help! Her leg is broken!"

"I'll be right there," he replied before turning back to face the woman one last time.

Before he could get another word out, she spoke first. "This is your party! Do something!"

"What's the problem?" Bixby asked.

The woman pointed a trembling finger at the inferno. "My son's still inside!"

Bixby swallowed hard. "Where?"

"I don't know! There was a loud boom, and the fire started everywhere. He panicked and ran from me and my husband! The guards pulled us out before we could find him..." she said, sobbing.

Outside the front door, the guards were holding back someone who Bixby could only assume was the father.

Everyone at the party, including Bixby's competitors, were listening to her shout in terror. Bixby slid away and made sure that Marin, Tipton, and her were tucked out of their sight before they spoke to each other once more.

"Final Boss Key," Tipton said as he pulled their answer card out of his jacket pocket and handed it to her.

"What is the final Boss Key?" Marin asked.

Bixby pulled as close to Tipton and Marin as she could.

"Yeah, it has to be," she said, smiling at his observation before turning to Marin. "The Phantom's riddle gave us locations of the small riddles, like keys in a video game. To get the Final Boss Key to solve the last riddle, we need all the little keys by finding and solving these riddles."

"But nobody said a riddle," Marin whispered before wincing in pain.

"This riddle is, 'Where's her son?' and to know that we have to unjumble the answers to the easier riddles," Bixby said as she scanned over her answer sheet.

Tipton twisted his mouth to the side as he looked at the card. "But these answers don't make any sense."

"Half of the easy puzzles were red-herrings for us solving Level Two, but they were the real answers for those people at the party trying to solve the Phantom's Riddle for themselves," she said. "Guests *did* have a chance to earn real money if they could figure out the other parts of the Phantom's Riddle."

Bixby then began to analyze her answers, and crossed out the ones like fireworks, music, fire, light, match, and all the ones related to how the fire started.

With the answers Bixby found on her own, and the two Marin gave her, it all came together.

"I know where he is," she said with no small amount of pride. Bixby hurried over and knelt next to the woman before asking a question soft and low. "Your son, does he like to hide when he hears thunderstorms or fireworks?"

"How would you know that?" the woman replied.

Bixby nodded. "Is that a, yes?"

"He usually goes in his closet," she said.

Bixby stood, nodding again. "He's in the kitchen. Probably the pantry, but maybe a cubby or closet."

"Got it," Daryl replied, looking impressed. "I'll get him. You all stay here."

"I'm coming with you," Bixby said.

"No, you're not," he said with finality. "It's too dangerous."

"I'm still coming," Bixby said, tearing a section of her dress with the intent of using it as a cover for her nose and mouth. She then turned to Tipton. "You ready?"

Tipton shook his head. "I'll only slow you down," he said. "Besides, someone has to stay with Marin."

"I'm not that helpless, thank you," Marin said.

"I get that, but you should still have someone with you in case the others try to hold you back from finishing," Tipton said bravely to Marin before encouraging Bixby. "And I know now is the time for Bixby to focus without any distractions from us," Tipton replied.

Marin agreed.

"Doc, take care of her and we will get the boy out!" Bixby shouted at the man in the grey suit. He nodded as he attended to Marin. "Whatever you need," he replied to her offer.

"Okay, stay here then," Bixby said. "I'm on it."

Bixby took off, quickly catching up to and falling in line behind Daryl.

Approaching the guards that had formed a line to try and stop them from reentering the blaze Bixby could see a small group of them huddled around the other two teams and Barnaby engaging in a large shouting match. Barnaby caught sight of Bixby and tapped Wesley on the shoulder, who then angrily shot a glance at Maggie who was now looking confused as to how Bixby could be out of the barricaded hallway.

Upon reaching the fortification of guards, Daryl simply plowed through them like bowling pins and Bixby followed through the hole he created.

Daryl had selected a window near the end of the building to climb as for the moment, it was free of flame.

"The kitchen is at the end of the hall, but stay low because the smoke will be bad," he said, helping Bixby through.

They crawled through the room, and Daryl tapped on the handle to make sure the door wasn't hot.

"Warm, but we are good," he said, turning the knob. The room filled with smoke in a fraction of a second. The initial rush of heat passing over them reminded her of when she was baking cookies and she opened the oven, putting her head near the door.

"We've got to be fast," he said as he began to bear crawl down the hallway.

Bixby kept in rhythm with the burly man. She was confused as to where they were going because she'd checked every door in that hallway, and none of them led to a kitchen. Come to think of it, she hadn't seen a kitchen the entire night they were there.

Near the end of the building, they reached a shattered mirror. There, Daryl paused and ran his fingers along the back of the frame until they found a switch. It took a moment for him to flip it. The mirror gave way from the wall and slid partially out of the way.

"The heat must have damaged this," he grumbled. Daryl pressed his shoulders against the heavily carved wood, and with all of his strength pushed the frame the rest of the way open.

"Hidden tunnels for the staff?" Bixby asked.

"It's frowned upon to have laundry carts and food orders being run up and down the hallway. So, this system helps us stay mostly out of sight," he said as they shimmied into the hidden corridor.

Seeing that the smoke had not yet been able to make it into the hidden passage, he returned the mirror to its closed position.

"Almost there," he said.

Daryl slowed to a stop as he reached the double-swinging doors of the kitchen. Looking through one of their circular windows, he lightly touched the one on the right. Immediately, he pulled it back and gave it a sharp blow of air.

"The fire made it inside," he said with a frown.

"Then there's no time to waste," Bixby replied.

Daryl nodded as he wrapped towels around his hands for some protection. "I know. You stay here. I'll be in and out before you know it."

"You know I can't let you do this alone," she said, wrapping her hands as well. "Besides, two people searching will be faster."

Before he could reply, Bixby plowed through the doors and straight into a gust of heat that whooshed up her entire body, delaying her only for a second.

Frantically, they each took a side of the kitchen and yelled for the boy to respond, opening every cabinet door along the way. Thankfully, the fire had yet to reach the cabinets. The ceiling, however, looked like it was about to collapse at any moment—its beams fiercely burning.

"Nothing over here," cried Daryl.

Bixby didn't reply as she opened more doors rapid-fire, nearly taking each of them off their hinges.

Turning the corner, Bixby opened a cabinet and caught a flash of what she needed to see. A large metal pot reflected a flicker of movement behind her. There was a cabinet slightly ajar and then closed again.

"Under the sink!" she shouted.

As if it were a race, they both converged on it.

Bixby reached the cabinet first.

"Please be in here," she whispered, ripping the cabinet open.

A little boy huddled inside who couldn't have been more than five years old. He glanced at her with big eyes and then began playing with the cans of food, practically ignoring her completely.

"None of that, lad," Daryl said, yanking the boy free and up into his arms. "Time to go see your mom."

Daryl pivoted and ran. Bixby followed, lungs burning, legs aching.

Once they got back to the mirror, Daryl set the boy down and heaved the frame open enough to escape. The boy held up his arms as if he were asking Daryl to pick him back up. Without complaint, he did as they raced into the smoke-filled grand hallway. The fire was everywhere at that point.

"We need to get to a window," Bixby said as she entered a coughing fit.

Daryl, thinking the same thing, barreled into one of the bedrooms. There, he set the boy down. He and Bixby then tried to get the windows open. None budged.

"We'll have to get to another room," Bixby said.

Daryl shook his head and pointed to the hall that was now completely consumed by a firestorm. "No time," he said. "This is our only option."

Daryl ripped a flat cap and a jacket off one of the bedposts before donning them both to protect his head and arms. He then turned to her and gave her a tip of the cap.

Cold chills ran up Bixby's spine. The man before her looked like the spitting image of someone else she knew.

"Harvey?" she said, voice barely above a whisper.

The whistle in the furnace room was indeed familiar, and now with the cap and jacket, Bixby couldn't help but to make the connection. For the next moment or two, Bixby tried to convince herself it was the smoke making her brain foggy, but she couldn't shake the feeling whatsoever that Daryl was indeed the younger version of Harvey.

"Hey!" Daryl shouted, grabbing her attention once more. "I'm jumping out to clear the glass. Once I'm through, hand me the boy."

Before she could blink, Daryl dove through the single pane of glass, easily shattering it and sending shards everywhere.

The move sprang Bixby into action. She spun around to grab the boy only to be frozen in place due to another surprise.

The boy didn't act like a boy anymore. And he certainly didn't sound like one, either.

"Bixby, there is something you must know before we leave this room," he said in an all-too-familiar voice.

Bixby cocked her head. "Cody?"

The boy nodded. "It is outside of protocol for me to talk to you at all during any part of the Riddle, but due to unforeseen circumstances outside of this level, Pinnacle Manor has been compromised. All current access to the Holo based on your traditional Launch Rooms cannot be trusted. With that said, I must implore you to continue to solve the Riddle: the fate of Holo, myself, and people we love depends on you continuing your quest. That is all I can tell you without violating the terms of the Riddle." The little boy pulled a small piece of paper from his pocket, and then his voice changed back to that of a child. "You'll need this to finish this level," he said, holding out an origami submarine.

Bixby reached out and took the artwork from him, turning it over in her hands to inspect its perfection. She was now baffled at the overload of information that she had received in a matter of moments: *What did Cody mean she couldn't trust Holo? And why was the man she called Daryl a spitting image of Harvey? Who were the people he spoke of? Was her family in trouble? Or someone else?*

In the brief moment of befuddlement, the boy was pulled through the sill by Daryl. Another loud crash of stone wall behind her brought her back to the urgent task of exiting the building.

Bixby carefully lowered herself out the window, trying to avoid the glass that was scattered on the ground below. Turning from the window she had scrambled out from; Bixby was shocked to see that both the boy and Daryl were gone, but with the newly formed instructions, the only way to get answers was for Bixby to finish the level.

Bixby cautiously and hastily opened the folded paper art to reveal one simple sentence:

Look closely: the key has changed.

Bixby could hear faint screaming coming from across the lawn, and Tipton waved at Bixby as he stood near the carriage driven by Arthur.

He must have pulled up while she was inside.

"Let's go!" he yelled, flailing his arms.

Though her feet were now blistering from the smaller sized shoes she was wearing, Bixby ran harder than she had ever run before. Reaching Tipton and Arthur, she skidded to a stop next to the carriage.

"We have to hurry! Everyone just left!" Tipton said, climbing in.

"How do they know what to do next?" Bixby asked, confused. She was the only one to go in and get the origami riddle.

"I have no idea, but maybe we can still catch them."

Bixby jumped in the carriage and looked around. "Where's Marin?"

"I don't know. She insisted that the couple in the ruby red outfits help her up to watch you run into the building, and then I looked back after you made it in, and everyone was gone!" Tipton replied.

"You were supposed to watch her," Bixby said.

"I swear we were all watching you race into the fire, and as soon as you disappeared, the other teams' carriages started showing up. Maybe Maggie took her," Tipton explained.

"I think she would have put up a fight against Maggie," Bixby said, certain Marin was on her side. Just in case she shouted up to her driver, "Arthur, scan the crowd. Is she here? She's in an orange dress," Bixby asked.

Standing up over the crowd, Arthur began to work. The whole process only took a few seconds.

"I am sorry to report that Marin is not here, and neither is her carriage" he replied.

"I hope she didn't trick us," Tipton said trying to sound optimistic at the potential that Marin was playing both sides.

Bixby clenched her teeth. "How long ago did everyone leave?"

"Five minutes ago," Tipton replied.

"Six," Arthur corrected.

"Can you make these horses go faster than normal?" Bixby asked.

"I'm sorry, Lady Timmons, but I can only keep them at the pace they told me to at the stable house," Arthur replied. Hearing his response, Bixby jumped back out of the carriage knowing that she wouldn't catch up to the other teams if Arthur wouldn't push the horses.

"Please, Arthur. They're way ahead of us," Bixby pleaded.

"You heard the stable boy. If I push them, they will stop on their own," Arthur argued back.

"Then we'll meet you at the sub," Bixby replied.

"Bixby Timmons! I hardly think this is the time for—" Arthur started to respond.

Before he could finish his sentence, Bixby flew into action.

"Trust me!" she shouted as she smacked the hind quarters of the horse.

Immediately, Arthur was thrust back against his seat and the coach tore off into the night.

"That was our ride," Tipton stammered. Bixby turned to her friend, looked deep in his eyes, and a smile crept up her cheeks. He was excited by her response, but was slightly regretting having to ask, "We are going to do something stupid, aren't we?"

CHAPTER 25
WITHIN REACH

Some of the crowd was still trying to solve the puzzle while others were taking a keen interest in the small saga that was taking place between Bixby and the other carriages that were taking off down the path. As Bixby raced to the stable with Tipton, she could hear people saying things like, "Why didn't we get a carriage?" or "Maybe they figured out the riddle?" Bixby didn't have time to tell them that they had no idea what they were talking about. All she could focus on was catching up with the other teams.

The stable hand was trying to keep the horses from panicking with all the commotion outside.

Bixby crashed through the barn doors and ducked into the last two stalls.

"You two shouldn't be in here," the man growled, looking up from his work.

"Uh, He's probably right, Bixby," Tipton said nervously, scared again knowing that this was one of her hair-brained plans. He watched her buckle buckles and pulls straps around the horse. She did say she went to horse camp as a kid, but he had no idea she was fluent.

Bixby stopped momentarily and faced the stable caretaker. "Do you know who I am?" she asked.

"I don't care if you're the Queen of England. You're not taking these horses," he replied, squaring off with her.

"Actually, you're not only going to let us take them, but you're going to go finish getting mine ready," Bixby said with a determined look in her eye.

The man huffed. "Excuse me? Who do you think you are? The Doc?"

"No, but he's the one who said I could use them," Bixby said before she leaned out of the stall door. She then cupped her hands over her mouth and shouted. "You said whatever I needed, right Doc?"

The stable hand joined Bixby at her side and leaned out as well to see the Doctor hunched over nearby, staring at the castle while it continued to burn.

"Sir?" the guy asked.

The Doctor, still in a haze, didn't turn to look, but he did respond. "Whatever she says."

"See?" Bixby said, crossing her arms over her chest. "There you go."

A split second later, Bixby was back in action, getting Tipton on his horse and her on hers.

Moments before they were ready to go, Tipton's horse began to nervously circle. "Oh man," he groaned. "I think I should've stayed with Arthur. I have no idea how to ride this thing."

Bixby tore slits up the sides of what was left of her once beautiful green dress, bounded up the two steps, and readied herself on the back of the horse in a stable labeled "Sonic Boom."

"Crash course, Tipton: pull the reins left to go left, right to go right. Lean forward a bit in the saddle and stay low on the horse. To slow down or stop, pull back on the reins, say 'Whoa' along with your horse's name," she instructed.

"What is my horse's name?" he asked flustered.

"Sound Barrier," she said, giving him a smile and a wink.

"That sounds like the name you would give a racehorse." Tipton's eyes widened, realizing what he'd just said while realizing the blue ribbons and trophies on the walls around him were not for how beautiful of a horse he was.

"Because he is," Bixby replied. She raised her hand over the stable wall. Tipton instinctively clamped down on the reins and leaned forward slightly as her hand came down on the hindquarter of a thousand-pound rocket.

"Time to catch up again," Bixby growled to herself, hating playing much of this Level from behind.

With a flick of her foot, she, too, lit the fuse and launched into the night.

Other partygoers lunged out of the way as each horse thundered past. They closed in on the front gate in an instant as they tore off through the night, but not before Bixby noticed a couple dressed in matching ruby red outfits. They were placing their answer card through a slot in a box at the base of the gate wall. As soon as the card went through the open slot, they too disappeared.

Did they just unlaunch? Bixby thought. For the first time she had made the connection that they were not at a real castle but instead in a hologram. She looked down at her arm, the one that had been burned, and realized that the only way that could've happened was if she had a Holo-Launch Suit on.

But when had she put one on?

She didn't know, and she also didn't have time to think about it, either.

The moon was bright and lit the path ahead, as the horse's hooves clapped loudly against the stone bridge.

"I think that's Arthur!" Tipton shouted from the lead horse.

On the ridge above them, Bixby could see the glow from inside a coach cresting over the horizon. After a few seconds, it was gone over the other side.

"We are in striking distance," she said to herself as the horse's hooves went from a clapping sound to a rhythmic thumping. They must have made the dirt road already as Bixby lowered herself closer to the horse and pushed on into the darkness.

The carriage ride from town into the castle at Shadow Deep was about an hour total. Knowing the time difference between when she sent Arthur ahead of them, and the time difference between Arthur and the other teams, allowed her to guess when they'd be able to break into a full sprint and take the lead.

Tipton tried to wave at Arthur as they pulled up alongside him. Realizing it was a bad idea to have both hands off the reins, he corrected his mistake swiftly as his horse continued to pull ahead of the coach.

Bixby slowed to hear Arthur yell over the sounds of hooves. "For the record, I do not approve of this!"

"How long did that take to catch up?" was all Bixby could think to yell back focused on the task at hand.

"You caught me in twenty-two minutes, Lady Timmons," he replied.

Once safely past Arthur's carriage, she tried to do the math in her head, but realized, like the Santa math questions, she was missing too many variables. All she knew was that it was going to be close.

"There they are!" Tipton shouted.

Being able to see their carriage lights made Bixby more and more confident that they could catch up, but what puzzled her was why she could only see two coaches' lights in the darkness.

The flickering fire lights of the small village of Shadow Deep could be seen in the distance as the horses kept pace. The sound of the horse's hooves made another unique clomp as they reached the edge of town. Bixby could see up the hill as two of the coaches reached the stables and disappeared.

"They're already inside," Bixby muttered as their horse darted up the cobblestone road.

Tipton frowned. "What if they ambush us in the stables?"

Bixby nodded, knowing it was a real possibility.

"I have an idea!" she said, bringing her horse close to his and then swinging over into a side-saddle.

"What are you doing?" Tipton squealed.

"Keep it steady!" she yelled back, calculating her timing. "I trust you!"

The next second she catapulted herself into the night air. Tipton clenched the reins with one hand and with a mighty arm, he pulled Bixby in tight.

"Great catch," she said as she slid behind him.

The pair raced toward the barn. The stable hands took note of the two and started to pull the doors open again to let the riders enter.

Inside, they saw Maggie and Penny standing in the middle of the entry, waiting.

"Oh man," Tipton said. "They're waiting for us."

"Yeah, well, we're not stopping to say hello," Bixby replied, putting her foot out on her former horse and guiding him in the direction of the stable.

The animal raced through the massive doors without slowing down, forcing Maggie and Penny to jump out of the way.

"Whoa, Sound Barrier!" Bixby cried reaching around Tipton, pulling the reins, and turning the horse towards the harbor. She eyed the pathway that led along the front of the barn and down towards the shoreline. Before Sound Barrier stopped completely, she continued directing his reins down to the waterfront and gave him a little kick to speed up the pace.

She figured a gentle gallop on a horse would be much faster than Maggie and Penny could run to the subs.

"What do we do next?" Tipton asked.

"I think the final riddle is on our sub," Bixby replied, relinquishing the reigns back to Tipton. "The origami puzzle said that the key had changed."

"The puzzle box?" Tipton confirmed.

"I think so."

The horse's metal shoes made a terrific rhythm on the cobbled streets as he made the final turn into the docks. Bixby could see most of the port from the upper street that was lined with onlookers when they arrived. Bixby was so focused on seeing when Maggie and Penny would make their way out of the barn that she missed the most concerning issue.

"You didn't see Barnaby at that stable, did you?" Tipton asked. "Whoa, Sound Barrier," he then commanded the horse as it reached the gate to the docks.

"No, why?" she asked.

He didn't have to answer the question, because it was obvious what he was hinting at.

"She wouldn't have," Bixby gasped looking at the harbor and only three submarines left docked.

"Looks like Marin finished first this time," Tipton said.

His words left Bixby sick to her stomach.

How did she get here so fast? was Bixby's first thought. She had about a million more, but she didn't have time to dwell on them because there were two competitors ahead of her and their dates lurking someplace nearby. They needed to get to their ship swiftly.

"Let's go," was all that she could reply as she dismounted the horse and helped Tipton down.

They quickly and quietly moved down the first pier. Every step they took, all she could think was that they were walking into another trap.

"I don't like any of this," Tipton said, putting words to those thoughts she was having.

"Yeah, me either," she replied.

Despite the feelings, they had no other way to go but forward to reach their sub. They reached the ship without incident and quickly hopped aboard. Their shoes clacked against the metal hull as they made their way to the ladder of the conning tower. At that point, Wesley suddenly made an appearance from the tower's landing.

"Never send kids to do a man's job," he said, smirking.

Bixby screeched to a stop, and Tipton nearly slipped off the side when he jumped back.

"Predictable," Bixby said with a snort.

"Maybe me making sure you don't get inside your sub is predictable, but that's not going to change the fact you're still going to end up losing," he said, shrugging.

"You'd waste all that time just to ensure that happens?" Bixby asked.

Wesley nodded. "Sometimes you have to lose a battle to win the war. That's the difference between you and me. You can't look past your next step." He looked like he was about to say something else when he perked and looked off in the distance. "Ah, there they are," he said.

Bixby turned to see Maggie and Penny running down the docks toward them. Bixby had some time to react, she knew, but it wasn't much.

"I'll follow your lead," Tipton whispered in her ear. "Ready when you are."

"We need to get back on the dock," she replied, retreating a few steps.

Wesley tilted his head. "Looking to run some more? Be my guest. Run back all the way to the castle if you like."

"Maybe," Bixby said, not wanting to show her hand.

As Penny and Maggie finally caught up and started down the pier they were on, Bixby waited until the very last moment before springing into action. She jumped off the dock, dragging

Tipton with her, and hit the frigid water. The instant the two resurfaced, she gave her order.

"Swim for the other sub," she shouted. "They can't get us once we're in!"

Bixby turned the two of them towards Wesley's sub and pulled Tipton under the water.

Wesley straightened, his face awash with confusion, but it only lasted a moment or two when clearly realized Bixby's plan. The rules never said which sub had to be used to solve the final puzzle.

"Don't let them get to that ship!" he yelled, diving in after them.

Maggie and Penny immediately pivoted and sprinted back the way they'd come, heading for the other pier where another sub was docked. Bixby knew before any of that happened, all three of them would likely beat her and Tipton to the other ship, especially since Wesley was a champion swimmer—something she knew from the profile she'd read back on Level One.

But she didn't have to race any of them there to win.

While they were all so focused on getting back to their own subs, Bixby had pulled Tipton under and once again reversing course. Beneath the cold, dark waters, no one saw the two return to their own ship.

Quickly, quietly, once they'd surfaced, Bixby pushed Tipton up, helping him grab the rungs on the side of the boat. Up the side of the sub they went. They'd just reached the deck of the ship when Maggie noticed where they were.

"They're back on their ship!" she yelled, changing direction yet again.

"Don't stop," Bixby said as they ran. "Almost there."

Tipton reached the conning tower first with Bixby right on his heels. They raced up the ladder, and although they had a head start, Maggie was closing fast.

Tipton reached the top and quickly disappeared.

"Don't let her close the hatch!" Wesley yelled.

Maggie nodded and came at Bixby even faster than she already was.

Maggie lunged against the ladder with a thud, narrowly missing Bixby's shoe. The brief miscalculation gave Bixby the few extra moments she needed to get up and over the lip of the sub before grabbing the hatch with one hand and the rails of the ladder with the other. As Bixby began her slide, she could see Maggie's enraged face come over the top of the tower, reaching out to stop the hatch from closing. The metal door came down with a crash under Bixby weight. It bounced a little as the four fingers Maggie tried to use to stop the hefty iron seal from shutting instinctively pulled free from the crushing force. Bixby could hear Maggie scream, as she sealed the latch closed.

"There," Bixby said, exhaling sharply before smiling with pride. "Home free."

Tipton, however, seemed to disagree. He shot her an angsty look.

"Yeah, we're here, but what about Arthur?"

CHAPTER 26
NO MARGIN FOR ERROR

Bixby raced to the bridge of the ship, ripped off her mask, and tossed it aside. She plopped down in the captain's chair and detached the cube from its resting spot.

"Hey! What about Arthur? We can't leave him out there with them!" Tipton yelled as he caught up.

Bixby pointed to the outside. "That Arthur," she said, "is not the real Arthur."

Tipton stiffened with surprise. "Huh? How do you know?"

"Two reasons. First, he wasn't approved to come in the Riddle with me when I entered names into the computer as a partner to launch in with," she said, now searching the cube for any irregularities.

"We're launched in?" Tipton asked.

"Your suit is a Holo-Riddle Suit, and your cubby is a launch room," she explained.

"We are in Holo?" he questioned.

"No record of a castle that doesn't exist, and yet we were there?" Bixby returned question for question as she rotated the key in her hands.

"Well, okay. Maybe," he stammered, thinking about the possibility. "What's the second reason you know he's a fake?"

"Only the people *inside* this level have called me Lady Timmons. The real Arthur always calls me Miss Timmons," Bixby replied.

Tipton pondered her logic knowing she was probably right.

She went back to studying the cube with her full attention, and Tipton remained silent.

Nothing stood out to her, and the more she looked it over, the more frustrated she grew. However, when the familiar scene inside the cube played out, and the lighting of the fireworks began, something did change. Instead of directing her to find the cube's home, a new message displayed:

It now read: HOW DID IT START?

"How did what start? The fire? The rest of the boss keys tell us that the fireworks started the fire!" Tipton blurted out as he raced over to the computer that had come to life with instructions for them to type their answer.

"No, stop!" she yelled.

Tipton froze just in time, and she directed him to the flashing words at the top of the screen.

"There's a five-minute penalty for any wrong answer," she said.

"But it *has* to be 'fireworks,'" he replied. "Right?"

"The paper said, 'Look closely: the key has changed.' The fireworks are the riddle, but I think something has to be different about this key," Bixby replied as she turned the cube over in her hand.

"Well, it is the last puzzle," he said, taking a spot next to her. "It can't be that easy."

"Exactly. You're a gamer and know that Boss Level Puzzles never are. This should be the hardest puzzle of them all, and we can't afford a penalty," she replied.

"Then what does the word 'it' refer to?"

"I don't know, but I am certain it is not fireworks," she said. After a moment, she started brainstorming out loud. "'It' could be opening the cube at Pinnacle Manor? Finding the sub?"

"The mayor greeted us, and made you give a speech?" Tipton added. "Or maybe putting the cube in the captain's chair?"

"None of that seems to be a perfect fit, though, because none of those would be part of the key changing," she said, getting more and more frustrated that she couldn't make out what type of puzzle this was.

He huffed knowing that he was no help to her solving riddles. "You've got this Bixby, I'll let you think," he said knowing she did better when she had time to herself. He went over to the ship's periscope and trolled the boats around them, while Bixby read the fireworks exploding over and over again.

"Uh oh," he soon said, backing away from the periscope. "You're going to want to solve that riddle really quickly."

Bixby sat up alert in her chair. "Why?"

"Because Greg is on the tower of his ship shouting at the other team. And now Maggie and Penny are running back to their ships," he replied. "Take a look."

Bixby dashed out of her chair and looked through the scope. She immediately saw Penny disappear below the deck of Wesley's boat, and Maggie was gingerly climbing the ladder of Greg's ship one handed while nursing her smashed fingers against her chest. Greg was shouting something to Wesley.

Bixby squinted trying to read his lips. "What's he saying?"

"I'll try and figure it out," Tipton said, moving for her spot. "You get back to the cube."

"Perfect," she replied, returning to the small object.

Bixby knew she may have only one guess, and she had to make it a good one. The fireworks were shooting off again and would soon playback. She was tempted to type in 'fireworks' as the pressure of the puzzle was starting to wash over her.

"What am I missing?" she asked herself looking over the scene again.

It took Bixby days to figure out the cube the first time. The weight of that thought made solving the cube a second time in a few minutes stressful beyond belief.

"Bixby, Greg is turning the castle around and looking at it from the front of the building and not the balcony side. Wesley is looking at the front of the building now!" Tipton called back.

Bixby spun the cube around and inspected the front of the castle.

She felt as if she were cheating by spying on Greg, but she didn't care knowing that during the entire Level she had been disadvantaged, held up, and outnumbered at every turn. This riddle had at no point been fair.

"Bixby, hurry. They're all getting in their boats and closing their hatches," Tipton said with a tremor in his voice.

"Where are you?" she pleaded with the cube.

"If we don't know, we've just got to guess and hope it's right," Tipton urged.

She was frantically turning the cube on every angle, but still nothing jumped out at her.

"There!" she shouted, catching a reflection from the miniature ten-foot-long mirror on the second-story hallway.

Tipton spun around, awash with energy. "What?"

"It was the Phantom. I can only see him briefly in the reflection of the mirror, and in his hand is a piece of paper. Most of it is scribbly lines, but there were definitely letters at the beginning," she impatiently waited for the scene to play over again to see him glide by the mirror.

"It's like a Seek-and-Find Puzzle!" she explained. "We had to find what was different and when we did, we would know to what 'it' in the clue was referring."

A few moments later, the fireworks finished going off, and the scene began again.

"There!" Tipton shouted.

They both desperately peered into the window to read the writing on the paper.

"Phantom's Riddle!" Bixby shouted the legible words out loud.

Tipton pulled out his soaked card from his pocket and slapped it down in front of them both. The ink was running down the page, making it hard to read.

"Time!" Tipton shouted, pointing to a smudged section at the beginning of the Phantom's riddle. "It has to be 'time.'"

Bixby shook her head. "No. That's not it," she said wide eyed and confident, slipping in front of Tipton at the keyboard.

Her fingers danced along the keys for a brief moment before she hit the ENTER key.

Nothing happened.

Not on the screen.

Not in the sub.

Nothing made a sound anywhere.

She slowly turned the chair to face the periscope.

"Did we do it?" Tipton whispered.

An ear-piercing groan ripped through the air. Before Bixby could react, everything went black. She couldn't tell if it was the lights going out or her body being slammed against the control panel of the sub. What she did know was that the ship had violently jostled, and her cheek was now up against the cold metal floor in the darkness as safety lights flickered overhead.

"Tipton?" she moaned, pushing herself up. "Tipton? You there?"

Her eyes started to regain focus in the dim light surrounding her. As she stood, someone beat heavily on a nearby door.

"Miss Timmons! Miss Timmons! Are you in there?" Arthur shouted from the other side.

Bixby was no longer on the bridge, but she recognized the four bland walls that surrounded her now. Bixby stumbled her way to the hatch. It took her a moment, but she managed to pull the steel handle up and the door opened.

"Thank goodness," she said, falling into Arthur's arms.

"Miss Timmons, I've got you now," he comforted.

Bixby nodded. "I'm...I'm okay. But where's Tipton?"

"Sit here and I'll check," he said, helping her get seated against the wall.

Arthur banged on Tipton's door, and eventually, he also emerged from his Launch Room.

"Bixby," he said, limping over to her and taking her side. "You okay?"

Bixby smiled. "Yeah. I'm good. You?"

"I've had better days," Tipton replied with a shrug and a smile. He looked as beat up as she felt.

"So, it wasn't 'fireworks' or 'time?'"

Bixby's smile broadened as she shook her head and thought about Cody's cleverness. "'Silence.' That was the first word spoken to get the crowd to hush."

Tipton pondered standing under the balcony in the darkness and hearing the word 'Silence' as it sent shivers down everyone's spines.

Tipton found himself smiling and nodding his head repeatedly at the realization that she was right. "I'm glad I am on your team," he said, knowing how much he did and didn't enjoy taking part in Level Two.

"But did we beat Wesley or Greg?"

Bixby shrugged as they both looked up at Arthur.

He shook his head. "I'm afraid I don't know either."

Bixby cocked her head, realizing that the sub they were in was not only moving but changing headings as well. "Where are we going now?" she asked, taking to her feet.

"I'm not sure of that, either," Arthur confessed. "I can only say with certainty that once you two unlaunched, the ship set sail."

Bixby nodded and pointed her feet in the direction of the bridge. "Any chance we've heard from Pinnacle Manor or Pippa yet?"

"Sadly, no," Arthur replied.

"Of course not," Bixby muttered, reaching the bridge to inspect the navigational map. She was trying to keep the worst of her thoughts pushed far away. She could immediately see the ship was retracing its steps along the coastlines.

She needed a moment to think, so she gave Tipton a task. It was her way to let him be part of the riddle of 'what next?' without getting in her way. "I think there's something wrong with this earring. Can you check it out?" she asked, pulling her earring from her ear and handing it to Tipton before spinning the Holo-Globe.

Tipton took a look at them, but he didn't have to look at them for long. His face soon soured. "Bixby, I'm not sure how to say this."

"Say what?" she asked, stopping her search of the map.

"When we built the Takos, there were three legs needed for this system to stand: the earrings, a satellite to broadcast the signal, and Harvey's system to help with the logistical things needed done.

"So, what is the problem?" Bixby asked.

She could tell that her prodding made him nervous because he began to ramble.

"Your dad and Harvey helped me route them through Harvey's system as a security failsafe. Pippa then hacked an unused Dragonthorp satellite to relay the signal to herself and these earrings. Any one of those three go down and the communications were lost," he explained.

"Tipton! Get to the point," she interrupted him, insisting on an explanation.

"What he means is that the Takos are working, and so is the satellite..." Arthur said, soft and somber.

She looked deep into Tipton's eyes and could tell that what he was about to say was not only going to be hard for her to hear, but also for him as well so she said it for him.

"Which means Harvey is gone," Bixby finished. "And Pippa."

Bixby drew in a long, deep breath. She could feel her skin flush with anger as she centered the map over where the ship was and selected a new course: home. The map asked her if she was certain she wanted to change course. Without blinking she reached up and confirmed.

What she'd find at Pinnacle was anyone' s guess, but she knew it wouldn't be good.

Not by a long shot.

CHAPTER 27
RUBBLE

Having nothing to do and everything to worry about was an awful thing. Bixby tried to eat, but her stomach was churning with anxiety. She then tried to solve puzzles in her head, but she already knew the answers to the enigmas she came up with. She found herself pacing, but the further away from the physical demands of the riddle she was, the sorer her body became. The logical thing to do was to try and sleep like Tipton was, but there was a small bit of apprehensiveness that going back into her room would launch her right into Level Three without her even realizing it.

She stood in her tattered dress knowing that she couldn't launch if she didn't have the Holo-Launch Suit on that had been disguised as a dress.

Bixby tied the door to her room open with a chain she found in one of the mechanical closets; she would have taken the door off completely so that it wouldn't seal closed creating a prepped Launch Room, but the hatch was welded on. She then locked herself in the bathroom.

Grabbing her old clothes from her bed and readying herself to wash up, Bixby recalled the leather book that should still be tucked under her pillow. Pulling it out, she could see that it was no worse for wear. Grandpa's journal made her smile as she locked herself in the bathroom, pushed her back against the corner walls, and slid down.

"That riddle was hard, Grandpa, and I don't even know if I made it through to the next level," she said.

She opened the pages and read some of the familiar words:

You are a Timmons: Rich in history, faith, and love. You were born a fighter. Nobody messes with a Timmons' faith, family, or friends without arousing the leviathan inside. Those loved by a Timmons will never feel a greater kindness from anyone else in this world. That is our name and how we live our lives.

Bixby read the words over and over again, but she didn't feel great about this riddle and how she played this time.

She had to be deceptive. She had to use force. She pushed her way into the riddle instead of waiting for her family, and she'd almost destroyed her relationship with Tipton by her selfish actions.

"You never taught us Timmons' to be any of those things," she said as a tear rolled down her face. Bixby didn't like who she was in Level Two. Even more so, she was scared that because she was all the things she never wanted to be, it was why she lost communication with her family and why she felt so terrible inside. The weight of her own disappointment sat heavy on her shoulders. Bowing her head in her knees she began to cry a cry that helped her sleep an awful sleep.

She didn't know how long she had slept, but the boat made another gentle, but noticeable, turn stirring Bixby from her slumber. She was still covered in the muck and the mire from the riddle as well as the streams of dry, ugly-cry tears on her cheeks. It was time to clean up and face what was coming. She set the leather journal on the sink, found the clothes she came into the ship wearing and took time to make herself presentable.

After giving herself a once over in the mirror, and admiring all of her Level Two bumps and scrapes in all their glory, she tucked Grandpa's journal away, hardened her emotions the best she could, and made her way back to the bridge.

"I'm glad you're awake, Bixby. We should be arriving at Pinnacle Manor shortly," Arthur said. She could see he was doing the math in his head.

"Is Tipton up?" she asked, realizing she hadn't checked on him.

"I am not certain that he is, but I know he hasn't been this way," he replied as the ship made another gentle turn.

"Let me know when we get there," she said.

The ship straightened its course, and Arthur also straightened. "I believe we're coming into Worthy Lake now."

"Can you take us up? Bixby asked.

Arthur nodded. "Of course. Wake Tipton, and I'll bring us up."

Bixby left the bridge and got Tipton out of his room. By the time he was up, and they were back in the hall, the submarine let out a small hop.

Arthur then shouted from the bridge. "We've surfaced. You can go up."

Bixby huffed a big breath as she reached for the rungs, climbed the ladder, pushed the lock open, and spun the screws to open the hatch.

Once out and on top of the conning tower, Bixby froze at the sight of Pinnacle Manor, unable to put words to it all.

Tipton joined her a moment later. His jaw hung open a few beats, but he did manage a few words. "Blue screen of death."

Pinnacle Manor was gone, looking indeed like it had suffered a digital death. Large sparks jumped from all over the clifftop. Countless blue holographic cubes that had been used to shift and create every aspect of her home lay scattered about, flickering on and off, while the smell of burnt electronics filled the air.

The ship grew closer to the secret port at Pinnacle as Bixby stood stoically waiting to discover the extent of the destruction and to find her family.

"I can stop the ship out here and—" Arthur started over the ship's loudspeaker.

Bixby shook her head. "No. Take us all the way in."

The ship pressed on. The bay doors hidden in the side of the shoreline started to go up, but with a large metallic shriek locked in position. Arthur managed to slow the sub enough to thud against the seized doors. Once it had stopped, Bixby raced down the ladder and jumped into the water. It was a small swim to the beach, and the cold water felt good on her body. She could tell that Tipton and Arthur had dived in as well.

While giving chase to Bixby, Arthur shouted, "The security pad is just on the other side of the dock. I should be able to get it in two minutes, if you would please not rush in."

The words hit Bixby like a baseball bat to the face. The last time Arthur had begged her not to rush ahead, she ended up launching the ship without her family. Though she was anxious to get inside, she had learned that going slow and gathering good information was way better than going in blazing with no plan.

"Two minutes," she agreed, slowing to let him pass.

Arthur moved swiftly, and once he reached the rock wall, he ran over to a keypad. Even from how far away she was, Bixby could see that its screen had been shattered. It didn't stop Arthur, however. He reached over to his forearm and lifted a small flap. Pulling a cord from the inside of his arm, he connected it to a port beneath the screen. His eyes fluttered back and forth rapidly as he went to work as if he were speed reading text Bixby wasn't privy to.

After almost a minute of simply standing there, Arthur reached up and disconnected himself from the system and made his way back to Bixby and Tipton on the beach.

"You almost ran out of time," Bixby said.

"But I didn't," he pointed out, showing that he was good for his word. "I have both good news and bad news. Which would you like first?"

"The bad," she replied without hesitation.

"There is no system left in this house. Not one bit," he replied.

Tipton's jaw dropped and his hands found the top of his head. "What do you mean nothing? There's got to be something, right? There can't be nothing, nothing."

"What I am saying is that whoever was here before us has either disconnected every wire from the system, or they took it all; hard drives, cables, servers, light capacitors, everything. The system you know as Harvey is not responding whatsoever."

"It's all gone," Bixby said knowing that was most likely the case. "What's the good news?"

"My system was built into my unit. Before we left, I backed everything up. I have most of the security programming and parameters stored right here," he said, pointing to his head. "That part of Pinnacle can be fully restored."

"What about my family?" Bixby asked, panic welling. "Where are they?"

"We can go look, but I don't see anything that would indicate that they are here," Arthur replied.

Bixby didn't ask any more questions, because she had enough information to rush ahead this time. Arthur tried to catch her as she darted to the stairs, but Bixby had a fire inside her that would have willed her to do any feat of strength or speed. She took the stairs two and three at a time as she went.

She burst through a door labeled, "To The Lighthouse." Bixby slid to a stop, hoisting her hands over her head to protect her from the sparks that flew from pulled cables overhead. The lights in the ceiling flickered on and off like a scene from a scary movie.

"Mom! Dad!" she screamed at the top of her lungs.

No one answered.

Bixby paused her frantic search when she barreled into the Launch Rooms and saw a number had been scratched into the glass of all the control panels. It was impossible to miss.

"One twenty-seven?" Bixby said, cocking her head.

Arthur came racing in a moment later. "Be careful!"

Bixby didn't reply as she dashed out and raced into the Great Hall.

She found it completely destroyed, too. Furniture was torn to bits. The mantle over the fireplace was ripped from the wall. Ornaments were smashed all over the floor, and the Christmas tree had been pulled down and partially burned in the fireplace.

Nothing had reset like it was programmed to do when Bixby entered the room.

A crackling and popping noise precluded sparks flying in the air. Bixby recognized immediately where it came from. Hucklebee sat against the foot of her dad's lounge chair, slumped over. The panel on the back of his neck had been pried open, and wires and fibers had been torn out exposing his gears. Miss Marmalade was at the base of her dessert cart near the corridor that led down to the bedrooms. She was in the same condition.

"They took their hard drives as well," Arthur said once he caught up and had inspected their bodies.

Bixby rushed over and pushed Hucklebee back against the chair. He looked back at her blankly.

"Can you fix them?" she asked, voice cracking.

"I'm sure I can, but Harvey was the only one who could uplink to the two of them. Without him, I can't do anything to bring their systems back up or reinstall their memories," he replied.

Tipton finally arrived but didn't say a word.

Again, numbers caught Bixby's eyes, these scratched into her father's favorite leather chair nearby.

"One twenty-seven?" she said curiously. She turned and scanned the room. The numbers were everywhere.

"Any idea what it means?" Arthur asked.

"No, but they're all in my dad's handwriting," she said.

Tipton twisted his mouth to the side. "He left you a riddle?"

"I think so," Bixby replied. "He knows me better than anyone else, which means he knew I would understand this riddle, and he put it everywhere knowing I would see his handwriting."

Bixby thought about the numbers some more before reaching into her waistband and pulling out her grandfather's journal.

"And he knew that I never left home without this," she said as she flipped the book open. It was the only thing that her grandfather left a copy for both her and her dad. "I think it's a page number."

With that, she flipped through the book until she reached the spot in the book and read:

Sometimes the only way to solve a difficult puzzle is to pause, experience something else that brings you joy, and then come back with a new outlook.

Bixby leaped to her feet and sprinted down to her room. She slid to a stop in front of her wooden door and reached for the latch. Riddles gave her comfort. It *had* to be what her dad was speaking about. Slowly, she gave the door a push, and as it opened to reveal her room, Bixby gasped.

All the gadgets and gizmos inside were completely crushed. Even the Cody Clock was lying in the middle of the pile of scraps. If it weren't for the indestructible glass cube that belonged in the Cody Clock, every last item in her room would be garbage. The mattress on her bed was slashed, exposing the stuffing and springs inside. The bookshelves were completely empty. As Bixby turned to look at the fireplace, she could see bindings still smoldering.

They had burned Cody's old books, comics, records, books handed down to Bixby by her grandfather, and even the record that looked like the poster in grandpa's study she had found days before. The slide picture above the fireplace was now jumbled back up and the secret passage to Cody's library was sealed shut. The only way to get back down to the library would be to solve the puzzle boxes again. That would be a problem as there was no way for Bixby to tell what gears went to what puzzle box.

"Someone pulled that shut," Bixby said. "Which means someone wanted to keep Cody's secrets hidden."

Bixby turned in place, feeling like she was missing something. She then walked over to her tattered bed, climbed up, and crossed her legs. She closed her eyes and focused on breathing in and out slowly.

Her stomach growled.

Her eyes flashed open as she again sprang to her feet, hitting the floor running. She didn't slow down at all as she flew through the Great Hall and into the kitchen. After nearly breaking the door off of the refrigerator as she opened it, she took inventory of the contents. Leftover mac-n-cheese, eggnog, cookies. Tucked neatly in the back corner was a freshly made turkey, cheese, and hot sauce sandwich. Bixby reached back and pulled out the plate and placed it gently on the countertop.

"What?" Tipton said, bursting into the kitchen. "A sandwich... the answer to the riddle is a sandwich?"

Bixby nodded. Peeling back each layer carefully, she found the answer to her dad's riddle tucked neatly between a thick layer of turkey and cheese.

"That's a titanium glass memory stick." Tipton said confidently.

"I think this is what my dad wanted me to find," she said as she grabbed a towel and wiped it clean.

"Arthur! I think you had better get in here!" Tipton shouted over his shoulder.

Arthur arrived at the kitchen and immediately took note of what Bixby had found. "I don't think I have anything in the house that will read that chip," he said.

"I think we do," she said before making for the exit. "Follow me."

Tipton and Arthur chased Bixby to the end of the hall. As they reached one of the last doors, Bixby ducked inside. The lights automatically turned on in the ten-bay garage. Untouched by the intruders was the non-threatening family minivan. Bixby dashed to the driver's side door and bounded in behind the wheel. Arthur took his position in her mom's co-pilot chair, and Tipton had to move one of the twin's car seats before he could shimmy in.

Bixby inserted the memory stick into the van's navigation system and turned on the van. She recalled her dad's passcode from the day they moved in, and the dashboard system sprang to life. A hologram of Harvey appeared on the console.

"Bixby, if you are watching this, you already know that your family is no longer at Pinnacle Manor. Please know I will bring them someplace safe, but from here on out, you are on your own with whatever team you formulate. The system is blocking all other protocols and will not let me record what is happening right now. This is the best I can do. I am, however, able to back up my system onto this memory stick. Also attached are the schematics of the hardware you will need to restore Pinnacle Manor."

Arthur quickly opened the port in his arm and linked into the van.

"I'm not sure who is trying to breach Pinnacle, but you must get my systems put back together. No matter what happens, do not stop until you solve Cody's Riddle. I'm terribly sorry. I must go. The security at Pinnacle is now compromised."

With that, Harvey was gone.

CHAPTER 28
CALLING T-NAT

One can live in a void for only so long—she was in the space between being knocked to the mat in a fight and deciding to get up and keep fighting.

In the midst of the silence of her head the contemplative wrestling began.

"I will bring them someplace safe," was the phrase that stood alone in her mind from all the rest of the data she had.

Was Cody in that same place?

All she knew was that her dad led her to the chip playing the message, and Harvey said that they must keep going. Everyone was telling her to get back into the fight.

Moving forward was where she had to hang her hopes.

"How do we rebuild Harvey?" she asked. "We've got no equipment, and no money. He couldn't have been cheap to build."

"I'm not sure," Arthur said with no small amount of hesitation. "We'll come up with something, though. I'm sure."

"May I?" came a request from the back seat.

Bixby turned around and faced Tipton. "May you what, Tipton?"

"Call for reinforcements," he explained.

Bixby and Arthur shot each other confused looks.

"And where are we getting those from?" she asked.

"I'll need Arthur to get me a secure channel through the van's emergency system," he said as he grabbed the back of Author's seat and pulled himself close. "You're going to like this. Promise."

Bixby gave him a look that could only translate to "Please?" but she didn't have to actually say it.

He reluctantly opened the flap on his arm, plugged it back into the computer, and pulled the touchpad from the center console before handing it back to Tipton.

"This is a one-time thing," Arthur said, regretting letting them see how he was able to access the ins-and-outs of computers.

Tipton tapped away as fast as he could.

"Ready?" he asked, turning the screen around.

Safe.
All is lost.
Need T-Nat.

"I assume whoever is receiving that knows what you are talking about?" Bixby asked, still a little lost.

"Do you trust me to ask for help?"

Bixby had hated letting others help, but the more she trusted those around her, the more she realized that it was nice not carrying burdens on her own. She nodded, knowing Tipton was the only person in the world that she fully trusted at this point. "Okay," she said. "Do it."

Tipton hit send. They waited together in silence for a soft ding and the follow up reply.

On the run.
L-3 bound.
Full deploy?

"Can you please translate?" Bixby asked, trying to decipher their code.

"Pippa is compromised and saying we're headed to Level Three," he said. "She's also asking if this is a full rebuild of Pinnacle Manor."

Bixby scrunched her face, how she was so certain. "Where is she, and how does she know that we are going to Level Three?"

Another ding came before he could fully answer her question along with a new message.

18DJMTDMK

"It's a short link," Tipton said.

Arthur held up a finger and after a moment to check if it was safe to click, he nodded. "Line is still secure. You can follow it."

Tipton clicked the link. An anchor for a small-town news station came online, and they were interviewing a young teen couple. Bixby drew to the screen as the interviewer began.

"I'm standing here next to Lilian and her brother Garrett who have won a large prize during a very secret Launch Room Riddle. Can you tell us more about your experience?" the reporter asked holding the mic to Lilian.

"We received an invite to launch in and solve a riddle that could win us up to ten thousand dollars. At first, we thought it was a prank, but our mother's medical bills have been getting pretty high so we thought we would take a chance," Lilian replied.

"I'm sorry to hear that," the reporter said. "Will this prize be enough to cover it?"

"It's not everything, but it will help our family greatly," Garrett replied.

"Now that you solved it, care to tell us what the riddle was and how you found the answer?" the reporter asked.

"It was Cody's riddle," Garrett said proudly.

"You're saying that you were in the famed Cody Dragonthorp Riddle?"

"We didn't know at first when we got to the masquerade ball. All we knew was that we were required to answer the Phantom's riddle," Lilian explained. "It had us stumped most of the night, but then a girl at the end gave us some information that helped us get the right answer."

The reporter reached up to her earbud, listened to something, and said, "We are now getting confirmation that this was Cody Dragonthorp's Riddle as it is now being streamed live on Holo-Connect," she relayed, and then turned back to the exclusive interview. "Any idea who the mystery girl at the end was that helped you? Was it Bixby Timmons?"

"No, but my new favorite color is orange," Garrett replied with a smile.

Bixby clicked the link off before the reporter could continue.

"Marin didn't beat us, she disqualified herself to help that family..." Bixby's voice trailed off as she grabbed the tablet from Tipton.

"She didn't beat us to the dock?" Tipton asked, making the connections to why her sub was gone. "Why would she do that?"

Get2PM Now
Bring Orange Girl

Before Bixby typed her last phrase to Pippa, she asked, "What is T-Nat?"

The question made Tipton excited to share. "It is a large shadow group of outsiders and hackers that have always been leery of Dragonthorp Inc. Before the Riddle, they were fringe people, but then they watched Level One and became your biggest fans. They call themselves The Timmons Nation."

Bixby was baffled by the idea that a group of people would be her fans, let alone help her rebuild the greatest house ever created. "How many are we talking?" Bixby asked.

"No idea. But I'd say it's an entire army, and they would come to your aid in a heartbeat," Tipton replied.

"They can help rebuild Harvey?"

"They can rebuild his system and then some, but you are the only one with access to a Titanium Glass chip that has Harvey's coding on it," Tipton said, pointing to the dash.

Bixby felt the corners of her mouth drop as angst took over. "How do we know we can trust them?"

"Because you're about to message the greatest hacker in the world, and the creator of it," Tipton said with a smile.

Bixby's jaw returned to clenched with fury at the idea of cheaters, kidnappers, saboteurs, and everything she felt Dragonthorp Inc. now stood for. If winning it all is what it will take to get her family back, it was time to pull out all the stops. She began typing her message to the leader of a secret society of rebels:

Get2PM Now
Bring Orange Girl
T-Nat Full Deploy!
Specs Upon Arrival

Staring at the words, so concisely written, Bixby spoke not as a phoenix, but as a leviathan, "We rebuild Pinnacle Manor impenetrable our own way. Dragonthorp Inc. will fear us from now on."

Acknowledgements

This book is for the advocates of people.

To the teachers who tirelessly pour knowledge into our youth.

To those in the hospitals and EMS who strive to preserve all life.

To the men and women of our arm services who defend our freedoms.

To those in the police or fire rescue who run towards when all others run away.

To those who speak up for the children whose voices are not heard.

To the pastors who guide the soul on paths of righteousness.

To the humanitarians seen and unseen, you are a great light.

And all others who advocate on behalf of people.

Because to serve others is to model humility, understanding, compassion, and it usually comes at a cost. In doing so one inevitably learns the depth of sacrificial love.

About the Author

Dwight D. Karkan is a man of puzzles, and he loves the challenge of a good riddle! Currently, his favorite puzzles and riddles are being a parent, husband, and youth pastor. Dwight knows we are all designed as a beautiful combination of awesomeness, uniqueness, passion, gifts, and talents, and the only way to get a little closer to discovering the answer of who we are is by engaging each other with love.

In 2019, Dwight's daughter Selah was diagnosed with Leukemia which has been their family's biggest puzzle yet! His hope for Bixby Timmons is not only to bring a light to students who want to do bigger things than they think they are capable, but also to help families who have been through a similar struggle. If you would like to know more about how Bixby is helping those in need, join our team on our Facebook Group "Bixby Timmons Series" or his website www.dwightkarkan.com

About the Publisher

Tiny Fox Press LLC
5020 Kingsley Road
North Port, FL 34287

www.tinyfoxpress.com